Dogpile

DOGPILE

Copyright © 2020 by individual authors

Book design by Thurston Howl; Thiger helped with edits.
Cover art by Vale © 2020

First edition, 2020. All rights reserved.

A Thurston Howl Publications Book
Published by Thurston Howl Publications
thurstonhowlpublications.com
Fernandina Beach, FL

Dogpile

Pet Play Stories for Furries!

Edited by Thurston Howl

A THURSTON HOWL PUBLICATIONS BOOK

Contents

Waggy

TJ Minde

The two of us cuddled in my bed, his swollen knot still buried in me. He could pull out, but we liked keeping the closeness for now.

My gray wolf, with his white-furred chest and belly pressed against my back, wrapped his arm around me and ran his claws along my furless chest.

"Tonight was great, Waggy. The meal was wonderful and so was the sex."

"I'm glad you liked it." His claws continued to scratch at my furless chest and worked their way down to my stomach. Yet he always stopped before the one spot I actually had hair on my body. "You realize you're the only one that can get away with that nickname, right Hayden?"

I nodded. "I remember. 'Wagner with a V.'" I giggled.

"Are you ever going to let that go?" he asked, nuzzling the side of my head.

I scratched the fur of his hip pressed against mine. "Nope. That's how you introduce yourself, so I have to use it every now and then." From the corner of my eye, I caught a flash of the white on his muzzle. "I was a little nervous when you invited me over. I was expecting some huge meal with all of your family."

Wagner chuckled. "I mean, they've already met you and don't care you don't have fur. You'd have nothing to worry about." He rubbed my cheek. "But, this was the first year in a while that we didn't congregate together. I still made tons of food, though. The wonders of the Feast Day for St. Nicholas."

"Well, I'm looking forward to the next few lunches I get to take to work. Though aren't there feasts like every other day in the Catholic faith?" I asked.

"Yeah." Wagner nodded. "But it's the only one that we do anything with. It's more the signal of the start of a tradition."

"And what does that have to do with today?"

Wagner's tail thumped against the bed. "Well, instead of giving gifts on Christmas, we give them around the entire month of December." He set his paws on my hips. "I'm gonna pull out, okay?"

After I nodded, he tugged his hips back, and I let out a soft moan as I was stretched by his knot again.

"Sorry, love." He ran a gray paw through my short black hair, and I melted back onto him. A second later, he got out of bed. I rolled onto my back to watch as he grabbed a box from his closet. "And to keep that tradition going, here's the first gift."

"Oh, Waggy." I sat up, grinning like a buffoon. Then, the smile slipped away. "But I didn't get you anything."

"Don't worry," he said, beaming back. "This is my family's tradition." Wagner nudged my shoulder. "Now come on, open it up." He looked from me to the box with excitement in his eyes.

I tore the paper off the package and found a set of black knee pads. The padding was soft at the point of contact with no plastic. I looked from the gift to Wagner and back.

"Knee pads?"

Wagner simply nodded.

"Trying to tell me you want more blowjobs so something?" I asked. "I mean, I can totally do that, but not tonight."

The smile on his face quickly turned to worry. "Oh no, no. Nothing like that." Wagner wrapped his arms around me. "I was doing some research and thought you might like these."

"Why? I don't get it."

The smile was back. "Well, a while ago, you said you wanted to try pup play." He pointed at the box. "And I read that crawling around on the floor is easier with knee pads. Don't need to worry as much about impact, and they don't need the hard plastic because they aren't trying to protect you from a fall."

I thought about it for a moment and hugged my wolf. "Thank you, Waggy."

His tail began to thump again. "I take it that means you like it?"

"I'm unsure right now, but I'm really happy you thought of me." I pressed my forehead to his. "But maybe we can try them out another night?"

Wagner moved the box and cuddled me again. "That's fine, babe. Maybe we can just rest here for a bit."

"What ever will I do with a big wolf on top of me?" I wrapped my arms around him, hugging closer.

"Cuddling, that's what. Also, I was thinking we might try sneak away for a few weeks around Christmas? I rented a cabin and was hoping you'd join me. Just the two of us." I could hear the apprehension in his voice.

"Oh Waggy." I nuzzled the side of his muzzle. "I'd like that."

Neither of us said another word, and the thump of his tail was the only sound in the room as we cuddled into the night.

The next few weeks leading up to the trip were calm. Wagner and I went on dates, had sex. Standard couple stuff. On my own, I tried crawling around on all fours and barking a bit. That took a few beers to work up to—more to help me get over my own worries. And, all things considered, what little I did was interesting.

The drive to the cabin was going smoothly, too. I got to play DJ while Wagner drove. And the higher we got in the mountains, the more the change in environments became clear. At first there were small patches of white, but the further we drove, the more snow we saw.

My gaze bounded from house to house. Snow piled high in yards while driveways and sidewalks were shoveled clear. Some homes had simple lights for the season. Others were decked out with full-on holiday scenes both secular and non.

"There are a lot more cabins up here than I thought," I said.

"What do you expect in the middle of a ski resort?"

"I don't know. I've never been skiing."

Wagner's tail beat behind his seat as it wagged through the tail hole behind him. "Then we'll have to change that. We'll certainly have enough time to do so. I promise, Hayden: I'll take you down the easy slopes at least once."

I let out a playful cheer as Wagner turned the wheel. Again I stared out the window. "Is that us?" I asked, pointing to the huge two-story building we crawled past.

Waggy let out a chuckle. "Not so much. That's the lodge. We're a few minutes from our cabin. It's a much more reserved dwelling." He rubbed the back of my head. "You're like me when I was a pup coming up here."

As I sat back in my seat, my cheeks warmed, and my gaze fell. But as I heard his tail thumb again, I smiled. "It's just all so new and exciting."

He chuckled again. "I know." His ears shot up. "Oh, and here we are." He pulled in to the well-kept driveway. No decorations adorned the exterior, but the place still looked cared for.

As I stepped out of the SUV, the crisp fresh air filled my lungs. The soft smell of the trees and other foliage floated about, while far-off birds chirped in the winter air. Purples and reds painted the sky as the sun had already begun to set in the distance. "Wow. I don't think I've ever been this far from a city."

Wagner clapped me on the shoulder. "Well, grab a bag and come on in. We'll get you someplace more suited for your standards."

"Hey," I cried, spinning in a circle to chase his arm. "What's that supposed to mean?"

Instead of replying, my wolf just laughed and walked on. I grabbed a bag from the back of the car and followed him. I knocked as much snow from my shoes as I could before I crossed the threshold into the cabin. And inside couldn't have been more different.

Along one wall was a large fireplace. The living room, dining room and kitchen combined to make one huge room with all the comforts of home. TV, heating, power.

"I thought we'd be roughing it a lot more," I said as I placed my bag on the floor.

A sharp *pop* came from the kitchen and, a moment later, Wagner walked over to me with two fresh glasses of red wine and a smile.

"And what's this for?" I asked, taking one of the glasses.

"Think of it as a vacation-house warming gift. Courtesy of my family."

I raised my glass to Wagner. "To a happy holiday away."

"Indeed," he said, as he touched his glass to mine and sipped. And once each of our glasses was lowered, he leaned in, wrapping an arm around me, and kissed me. A simple, gentle kiss, pressing his muzzle to my lips.

I couldn't help but chuckle. "And what was that for?"

"For being cute." He winked. "Why don't you take that and go start unpacking? The bedroom is back there." He pointed to the only other door across the room. "I'll get the last of the bags and join you."

"Okay." With the stem of my glass in one hand, I grabbed my bag with the other.

The bedroom was just as nice as the rest of the place. A large bed filled the space, flanked by two matching dressers. A long mirror hung across from the bed, and another door led to the attached bathroom. Setting my glass on "my" side of the bed, I began to unpack. Halfway through the second of three drawers—and a third of the way through the glass of wine—I heard Wagner in the living room as he started a fire in the fireplace, then came my way.

"Warming up from the cold?" I asked.

"Didn't you hear? Baby, its cold outside." With a spring in his step and smelling pleasantly of smoke, my wolf walked over to "his" side of the room and set a small, decorative bag on the bed and began to unpack.

"What's that?" I asked, nodding to the bag. It was covered in pine trees dressed for the season and a large red bow near the top.

Wagner's tail began to wag. "Gift number two."

"How many are there total?" I reached for the bag but didn't open it yet.

My wolf shook his head. "You'll have to wait and see."

I shook my head with a smile. "And what's this one celebrating?"

"The longest night of the year: the winter solstice. Now go on, open it." His full attention was focused on me as I reached for the gift.

A simple piece of tape is all that kept it sealed, and that was broken easily. I pulled out piece after piece of tissue paper until I found a small bundle wrapped in more colorful paper. Tearing it off, I was left with two boxing glove-like mitts. They were lightly padded with a stylized paw pad near one end.

"What are these?" I asked.

Wagner walked over to me. "They're mitts. For when you want to play as a puppy. It takes away a bit of the control."

My face flushed again, and I held them in one hand and sipped from my wine.

"You okay?" my wolf asked.

I emptied my glass and nodded. "Yeah. Just…nervous."

"Why's that?"

"Not sure, honestly. Maybe worried I'd upset you?"

Wagner stepped around to my side of the bed. "You don't have to put them on if you don't want to."

"I'll put them on only if you stop me if I do anything offensive." I paused, looking from the mitts to Wagner, his gray tail gently wagging. "It's also exciting." My voice became quieter. "Sorta taboo. So it's thrilling." My head buzzed. From the wine or the kink, I wasn't sure. But I smiled nevertheless.

"Wanna try them on?"

"Yes, sir," I whispered, as the submissive feelings began to take over.

He smiled. "You have your kneepads, right?"

I nodded.

"Good boy."

My hips swished as I tried to wag a tail that wasn't there.

"Put them on, then take your shirt off. After that, you can

meet me in the living room, and we'll put these on." Wagner took the mitts from me and left the room.

My heart beat hard as I pulled the kneepads from my bag. I sat on the floor as I slid them over my jeans. After I straightened the fabric out on each leg, I sat back and removed my shirt. With the article removed, I could feel myself letting go more.

I ran my knuckles over the small patch of chest hair I had before giving my head a gentle shake and made my way to the living room. I stood along the edge of the room, keeping the wall beside me. Closer to the fireplace, Wagner sat on the couch, watching and waiting. Beside him were the mitts.

As we made eye contact, I held my arm and dropped my gaze.

"Pups don't walk," Wagner said. Hearing the unspoken command, I moved to my knees. He then leaned forward and curled a digit towards himself. "Come here, pup."

I gave a small nod as I crawled forward. Tension built in me the closer to my wolf I got. This larger, more natural canid meant so much to me. I was worried I'd upset him.

Or let him down.

I stopped again a few feet from him. While the warmth of the fire drew me closer, apprehension stopped me, and my gaze fell again.

Wagner didn't move for a noticeable time, and I continued to look at the grain in the hard wood floor. My wolf let out a sigh, and I flinched and closed my eyes as I heard him slide from the couch. Not sure what to expect, I waited. For a strike, a scolding. Anything.

Instead, Wagner cupped my chin and tilted my head up. "You okay, buddy?" He pulled my gaze to his, and the worry was clear in his eye.

Seeing him care so much made it all better. I knew I could trust him. If I crossed a line, we could talk about it. He cared. I leaned forward and wrapped him into a hug.

"Hey, it's okay," Waggy said as he hugged me back. "You have nothing to worry about. I'm here to try and help you, okay?"

I nodded against his neck before a sniffle escaped me. A moment later, I sat back on my haunches.

With his tail moving from side to side, Wagner slid a paw along my chin and scritched behind my ear. "You okay to continue?"

I tested out a *bark* of agreement. With a smile, my wolf leaned back to the couch.

"Paw," he said, holding the glove open to me.

I balled my fist and pushed it into the mitt. And after Wagner set the buckle in place, we repeated the process for the other "paw." With both my fists bound, it was easier to walk on my hands. The padding protected my knuckles.

Waggy reached out a paw and scratched me behind the ears. "Good boy."

Hearing that made me smile from ear to ear. I leaned into my wolf's paw, happy and safe. After a while, we sat by the fire, my head in Wagner's lap and him running his dull claws over the same places against my scalp again and again. It was heaven. And like that, we cuddled, enjoying each other's company throughout the evening.

The next day, true to his word, Wagner took me skiing. And it was a blast. I didn't get much further than the bunny slope, but still, it was great. My wolf taught me how to move and took me down the training hill many times. And I only fell about a dozen times.

I was having so much fun that I didn't realize how much of a workout it was until we got home that evening. I showered and lay down on the bed for a moment, and I was out like a light.

Because I conked out so early, I woke before my wolf. I made some coffee and eggs, waking Waggy with wonderful kitchen smells. We spent the rest of the day inside. I lounged on one end of the couch reading a book while Wagner lay on the other with a sketchpad in paw and the fire keeping us both warm.

As the evening wore on and it got closer to dinner time, Wagner put his art equipment away and puttered around the dining room.

"Need any help, hun?" I asked from the couch.

He shook his head. "Nope. Just setting up for dinner." He placed two candles on the table and lit them.

"Mood lighting? We've never had that before." I sat up as he struck a match and put the flame to the wick.

"Patience, Hayden. I'll let you know when it's time." He shook out the match. "Why don't you start up some rice for us?"

I kicked my feet and sat up. "I thought you didn't need help?"

"But it will stop you from askin' about the candles, yeah?"

I rolled my eyes. "Is there a rice cooker, or am I doing this in a pot like a heathen?

"I don't know about 'heathen,' but I think you'll manage." He said as he pushed a glass of white wine into my other hand.

I sipped the drink before searching around the kitchen for the tools I'd need.

Through half the bottle, my wolf and I worked to make a light meal: rice, green beans and seared fish. We each took a plate and a freshly filled glass to the table and sat across from each other.

"Okay, now will you tell me about the candles?" I asked, grabbing my fork.

"Actually, can you wait on that?" Wagner nodded to the utensil. "Today is another tradition."

I set my fork beside my plate and waited.

Wagner just smiled. "It's okay. I didn't tell you. Today we celebrate PersonLight."

"What's that?" I asked.

"It's a day for people to come together and show that we can be the light in the darkness—like the candles at the table, or the fire behind us. It's a day to remind us that hope for the future comes through our capacities for reason and passion."

"That's really nice." I reached a hand to Wagner's paw. "I know I have a passion for you," I said with a wink.

Waggy's tail swished from side to side as he squeezed my hand back. "And you bring hope into my life. You are something that makes me happy to wake up each and every day."

I couldn't help but smile. "So these are more reminders for the holiday?" I asked nodding to the flames at the table.

"In a way." Wagner nodded. "My family always tried to limit use of artificial light today." He grabbed his fork and cut into his fish.

"So far, this has been the most religious sounding holiday that your family has celebrated," I said.

"It's from a philosophical way of thinking, not religion. And my family liked the message and added it in."

"So with this being another special day, does that mean another present?" I asked.

His ears perked. "You're starting to catch on. But one thing at a time. Let's enjoy our meal," he said, picking up his fork.

"Yes, sir." I lowered my head acting upset. A breath later, I dug in. And it was really flavorful, seasoned with simple herbs and pepper.

After the meal, Wagner directed me back to the couch where we had more wine and cuddled there by the fire, enjoying each other's company. My wolf kept the holiday spirit going as we talked about out hopes and dreams for the future—both for ourselves individually and us as a couple—and how those around us could help us closer to them.

As the night wound down and another bottle of wine was opened, I began to lean against Waggy, nuzzling him and whining for attention.

"Okay, hint taken. Let's get you into gear." He pushed me up, and I let out a *yip* of excitement and pulled my shirt over my head.

"Hey, this isn't the place for that." My wolf had to direct me into the bedroom to change.

Wagner closed the door, and I pulled the knee pads and paws from my bag. "Hey, Hay?"

I turned to him.

"In my research, I heard that some human-pups like to be wearing less while in headspace, as it can be more sensual feeling touches and things all over your body. You wanna try being in your gear and underwear tonight?"

My ears warmed—from the wine or the eroticism of the suggestion, I wasn't sure.

"Okay," I said, turning around to unbutton my pants.

When they fell to the floor, Wagner let out a huff of excitement. "Wearing *those* I see."

I looked over my shoulder; my wolf was staring at my bare ass, exposed through my backless faux-leather boxer briefs.

I smiled and wiggled my rump. "I packed a few things for you, too." I set my gear on the bed. "Do you want to help me get this stuff on?"

Wagner nodded. "Have a seat on the bed." As I did as he commanded, he grabbed the first knee pad and slid it over my foot. "Paw here," he said as he tapped his shoulder.

Having my foot called such sent a submissive chill down my spine, but I still did as he commanded with a smile. Bracing myself against his shoulder, he slid the protective covering over my flesh and set it in place. He then grabbed the other and repeated the process.

"Floor," he said. With a snap of his digits, he gave his next command: "Sit."

Right away, I slid down from the bed and landed on my knees with a protected *thud.*

Wagner held out his paw, and from the way he asked—no, commanded—I knew what he wanted. I placed my paw—wait? Yes *paw*—in his. A moment later, he had both my fists secured in my mitts.

Wagner snapped his digits and pointed to the floor again. "Stay."

I let out a whimper as I settled on my haunches and watched as my wolf walked back into the living room. I sat there, shifting, wanting to be close to him. My muscles twitched, aching to push me forward.

"Okay, come," Waggy called.

With as much speed as a body on all fours could move, I charged into the living room. My wolf was sitting on the couch, and I jumped up, setting my paws on his thighs and pressing my face to his chest, nuzzling up to his neck whining.

Wagner laughed. "You were a very good boy." He cupped his thumbs under my ears and scratched at the back of my head with both of his paws.

I wagged my rear in the most dog-like manner I could.

My wolf kept my head in his paws and pulled me back to meet his gaze. "Think my good boy can do it again?"

I gave a new whine before a two-syllable bark, nodding my head.

Waggy's tail thumped against the couch again. "Okay. Now give me another handsome sit."

With a yip, I scooted back from the couch and rotated a quarter turn. I kept my back straight, paws forward, head up.

My wolf patted my head. "Good boy. Now wait here."

As Wagner took his first step away, I whined and reached a paw out to him.

"No." He pointed back at me. "Wait." His tone was firm and commanding, and I set my paw down with a sigh. My wolf continued to stare at me for another breath before walking back to the bedroom.

And I waited.

I could hear him shuffling around, but I couldn't tell what through. "Aroo?" I tilted my head even though he couldn't see him.

"Wait, pup," Wagner answered. "Almost ready."

With a short, happy bark, I started wiggling my rear in excitement.

Waggy let out a short whistle. "Okay, come here, pup."

Again, I awkwardly charged forward into the room. As I crossed the threshold, I saw my wolf sitting cross-legged at the head of the bed, tail swishing, with a short box in his lap.

I set my chin on the edge and tilted my head, looking from my wolf to the box and back.

"Get up here, pup," he said with a wave of his paw.

I rose onto my feet for a moment and tossed a knee over the edge, scrambled up, and sat at the foot, opposite of Waggy.

Again, I looked from the box to my wolf.

"Go ahead and open it," he said, placing it in front of me.

I tried to set my paws against the sides of the box, but I couldn't get a grip to keep it in place.

Wagner chuckled. "Here, let me help."

As he held the sides, I barked a thanks and nosed the lid off. Inside was another piece of gear: a slender curved tail printed to look like it had fur. At the end was a thick bulb with a wide base to keep it in place.

My rear wagged as I jumped forward and nuzzled my wolf with excited yipping yodels.

"Hey, Hay!" Waggy said as he pushed me back, laughing at my excitement. "Down boy. I'm glad you like it."

I sat back on my haunches, still wiggling my rear, and looked from the tail to my wolf.

"Want me to help get it in?" he asked.

I pushed the package towards my wolf and turned around, pressing my head against the mattress and looking back showing him my exposed rear.

"I'll take that as a yes." Wagner set a paw on my right cheek, then the left. He tucked his digits under the elastic edge around my backside. As he spread my cheeks apart, I felt his warm breath before his muzzle slid between my cheeks.

I let out a soft moan as his tongue ran across my entrance. I always loved it when he rimmed me. And in this head-space, it wasn't different. As he worked my muscle, encouraging it to relax and let him in, Waggy moved one paw from my cheek and dragged it between my legs, over my growing bulge.

"I see you like that, pup," he said, groping my length and sack.

I nodded my head, whining in need.

"You think you're ready for the lube?"

With a smile across my face, I shook my head wiggling my hips more.

Waggy chuckled. "Okay. But you owe me later."

I nodded and barked in agreement before he pressed forward, rimming me again. His warm, wet tongue pressed against my entrance and, with his paw's additional distraction along my shaft, the muscle relaxed. As his tongue entered me again, I couldn't help but let out another moan.

Wagner chuckled, his warm tongue still in me and his breath hot against my ass. A moment later, he pulled back. I whimpered.

"You're relaxed enough, pup," he responded with a soft smack on my rear, reaching for a container of lube and poured some onto his first two digits. "Roll over," he said.

I did as my wolf commanded, exposing my belly and bulge to him. I brought my arms close to my chest and kept my knees spread in a submissive posture.

"Good boy." He set his dry paw on my shoulder and kissed me. I could smell my own musk on his fur, but I could ignore it. Our tongues danced in the passion of the moment. His other arm lay across my groin as he pressed the slickened digits between my cheeks.

I moaned into the kiss as he stretched me. Wagner slid in and out of me, pressing against my prostate again and again. My heart beat in my chest, and my cock throbbed in desire as he worked. Pre dripped from my tip, letting it slide against the inside fabric of my underwear.

With his tail hitting the bed again and again, my wolf broke the kiss and removed his digits from me. "I think you're ready. Back on your knees, pup."

With another whine, I did as he said. Again, I pressed my head against the mattress, rear up and knees spread apart. I closed my eyes in anticipation, not sure what to expect.

I heard a second *click* of the lube bottle followed by the rustling of tissue paper. And a moment later, I felt the bulb of the silicon slide between my cheeks. As Wagner pushed and twisted it, I felt the toy spread me. All the while, my wolf's paw returned to the tent between my legs. Breath by breath, the toy widened my entrance. Discomfort and the familiar pain of a larger toy pulled me, but Wagner's paw aided in distracting me, changing the sensations to pleasure. As I crossed the thickest point, I gasped and the rest slid in with ease.

The base stopped any more of the tail entering me, while the bulge was large enough on its own to keep in place without much worry. I opened my eyes and, without moving from my current position, wagged my rear from side to side.

Unlike the previous times, there was more weight behind the motion; the tail in me gently smacked from cheek to cheek. I couldn't help but smile.

"You like it, pup?" Wagner asked again.

I popped up and turned towards him. I gave a quick nod before I dropped my paws forward and curved my spine, raising my rear to the air.

"Now we can both be waggy," my wolf said.

I wagged my tail harder from side to side again as I batted at my wolf's knee.

"And now you wanna play?"

I barked in affirmation and wagged harder.

"Well then, it's a good thing I have a puppy toy right here." He leaned over the side of the bed and grabbed a rope bone. "Go get it!" He threw it into the living room.

And I scrambled from the bed and charged after it, feeling the pleasant weight behind me all the while.

Christmas Eve was another quiet day. The slopes were closed, and we didn't want to bother the shop keeps. Why keep others from their family if we could avoid it?

Instead of staying inside, though, Wagner led me to an open Christmas tree farm a short hike away. Together we picked out a tree and worked to cut it down and dragged it back by sled. While I made us lunch, he set up a tree stand. And after we ate, we proceeded to decorate it: tinsel, cranberries, popcorn, candy canes and a few simple glass bulbs.

It was so pretty.

That night, I stripped to my underwear, got into pup gear, and we played a little more. After the tail was in, we played fetch again. Though I preferred the cuddling and closeness, it was fun playing with my wolf like this.

Not that we didn't have fun doing other things. It was moreso the fact that I didn't have to really think. Waggy was able to give orders and let me be silly and playful.

When Wagner took the toy, he tossed it over near the tree,

and it slid under the branches. "Go get it, but mind the pretties," he said, specifying the glass bulbs.

I hurried over to the toy. Because of how far under it was, I didn't want to risk knocking over the tree. So, instead, I reached for it with my paws. Little by little, I was able to pull it towards me.

So engrossed with getting the toy and bringing it back, I turned right around once it was in my mouth. I felt a pine needle or two along my bare side, and I yipped, scooting away. At the same time, my tail swung closer to the tree, and there was a rustle of branches following by a loud crash.

With a louder bark of surprise, I dropped the toy and scurried away and moved by the fire.

"Hayden," Wagner called.

By the tone of his voice, I could tell a bulb broke. I fucked up. And in my worry, I lost the head space. "Shit, I'm sorry, Wagner. I'll replace it. Let me get a dustpan." I began to rise.

My wolf turned to me and pointed. "Sit," he said with a firm tone.

With the command, I slid closer back to the puppy mindset and sat back down on my haunches. But I was still worried and felt bad.

I watched as Wagner went into the kitchen area and grabbed the broom and dustpan, then proceeded on cleaning the shards from the floor and surrounding area.

Once the glass was disposed of, my wolf came over to me. "Up. Pup style," he clarified.

I held my paws close to my chest and balanced my weight over my knees and legs as my gaze was locked on his knees ahead of me.

He looked around me closely before looking at me again. "Any glass get on you?"

I shook my head. The warmth of the fire kept me comfortable, but I was still worried.

"Paw," he commanded.

Once I set it in his, he examined the leather and cuff, then moved down my arm. He let go of me. "Other one."

And again, he examined me. Then my torso and back, then rear and finally my legs. "I don't see any glass on you." He cupped my cheeks. "You worried me, pup."

I looked up at Wagner and tilted my head.

"It's my job to worry about my pup." He pressed his forehead to mine. "And I care a lot about you. I didn't want you to get hurt. I don't care about the broken decoration. There are tons more where that came from."

He then licked my nose with a smile. "Besides, pups don't talk."

I couldn't help but let out a small giggle before nodding.

"You want to play some more?" Waggy asked.

I shook my head. Instead, I curled myself against his lap and nosed his paw.

"Pets?" he asked.

I nodded.

"I think I can do that," he answered. And that we did for the rest of the night.

Christmas day was just as quiet. It started with a small service at the church nearby and was followed by a community brunch. Both were attended by those with and without fur. It was all a simple affair, but nice. Wagner introduced me to some of the other established regulars like his family. Everyone I met was wonderful and polite.

When we got back to the cabin, Wagner started a fresh pot of coffee, and I snuck off to the bedroom. When I returned, my wolf had poured two fresh cups and had them on the table.

I set a package beside the mugs and slid it closer to him. "I know your tradition is not to do gifts on Christmas, and I respect that, but I wanted to get you something."

I looked from the box to Waggy. He sat there, smiling.

"So, I hope you don't mind, but I still have something for you to open on Christmas." I wrung my hands in front of me, nervous both in the situation and if he'd like it.

Wagner set his cup down. "Hayden, take a seat. Have some coffee." He pointed to the chair beside him, and I sat down. My wolf then grabbed my hand. "Honey, there's no reason to be so nervous."

"I know, but I worry I'd upset you by ignoring your tradition."

"Hay, you aren't ignoring the tradition. You just acknowledged it. But there is no relationship rule here that says you have to follow every tradition I do. Are you going to start licking yourself clean?"

"I mean, if I could, I may never leave the house some days."

Wagner scoffed. "Please. That isn't all it's cracked up to be," he said as he grabbed the package.

The simple ribbon came off quickly, and the lid followed it. The first thing he saw was a case about the size of a large hardback book with a handle at one end. When he lifted it out of the box, my wolf noticed a new large sketch book under it.

"Oh, thank you. I really like this material," he said, pointing to the book.

I nodded. "I thought that's what you were always drawing on it, but I never saw you work on larger things. And I wanted to make sure you had the chance."

He then opened the case. Inside held a large number of different mediums. Pens, pencils, chalk, coal and many other tools of the craft. "Wow, I've wanted to try working with some of these before but never had the chance."

"I thought I heard you say something like that."

Wagner walked over to me and pressed his forehead to mine. "Thank you, Hayden."

"You're welcome." I kissed the muzzle in front of me. "And merry Christmas."

"Merry Christmas," he replied.

The next morning, while I scrambled eggs, my wolf cracked some himself. He said eggnog always tasted better after sitting for a few hours. He had me try a sip before, then after lunch. And he was right.

I drank the spiked nog the rest of the afternoon while reading. And by the fourth cup, I had developed a gentle buzz.

I set my book on my lap. "You know something I've

noticed? I pup-out more after I drink," I said, sipping from my fifth.

Waggy didn't look away from his sketchpad. "Is that a bad thing?"

I shook my head. "No. Just an observation. At first, it helped me relax and allow myself to do it. After these past few days, it almost feels more like a trigger, and I'm more likely to bark and stuff right now."

"Do you want to gear up?" He set his pencil back in the case then grinned at me. His tail began to thump against the couch.

"I'm starting to think you like this almost as much as I do."

His tail thumped faster. "It's dominant, yet soft. It gives me a chance to care for you in a new way. And I like taking care of you." He sat up and turned around, lying on me. "I can tell you enjoy it a lot."

"Yeah." I nodded, wrapping my arms around him and scratching at his chest fur under his shirt. "I can be more playful when I pup. And, if I wanted to, I could probably be more childish. At least once, I pondered knocking over a cup of water you had."

"And I would have beat you." Wagner wrapped his arms around my neck.

I chucked. "I know. And I would have deserved it. But that's something I can do as a pup that I can't do in my day-to-day. I don't have to put up with getting yelled at and can just have fun. When I broke that bulb, I started losing the headspace because my responsible adult-mind kicked in. And I was also worried you were going to be upset."

"But I wasn't, Hayden." My wolf rubbed under my chin.

"I know," I said hugging him tight. "Okay, enough serious stuff." I booped Waggy on the nose, and he nipped back at me just as playfully. I gave a small yip then giggled. "Help me change?"

Wagner nodded. "Sounds like a plan." He helped me up from the couch and guided me into the bedroom where we began our ritual. I stripped down to my underwear—a gray jockstrap today. Then he helped me put on the kneepads, then paws. After that, he teased and stretched my rear, prepping me for my tail.

While I enjoyed his attention, I looked back and noticed he was starting to pitch a tent in his jeans. With a whimper, I attempted to paw in the direction of his growing bulge.

My wolf noticed my paw and stopped rimming me. "You wanna do that in gear?"

I nodded my head.

"We'll see what we can do. But first, we gotta finish getting you ready."

I ruffed in understanding and rested my head against the bed. After more attention, he was able to get the tail in place.

Once my gear was on, he let me up. After I turned around, I pressed my nose between his legs and nuzzled the warmth. I felt his shaft throb as I gave him attention.

"Hey, pup, what do you think you're doing?" Wagner pushed me away.

I scooted back on the bed, giving my wolf space. Still, I wagged my tail, staring from his bulge to his muzzle and back, licking my lips all the while.

"You're a horndog today."

I barked in agreement. Sitting up pup-style, I showed him my own erection straining against my jock.

"I see it, don't worry. But you gotta wait. Besides, we can't play yet."

I sat forward with a needy whimper.

Waggy rose from the bed, tail swishing from side to side. "Wait here a moment."

My head tilted as my wolf walked out of the room. I barked to him in question, but all I heard was a chuckle in reply.

Moments later, he returned carrying another box; this one much taller than the last.

"Happy Boxing Day." He set the package in front of me, then waved to it. "Go on, open it."

I nudged myself forward and held the package between my knees and lifted the lid. Pert, black leather triangles poking up around dozen of pieces of tissue paper. I stared from the box to my wolf.

He was smiling from ear to ear. "Go on, tip it over and see what's inside."

I knocked the box over and shook everything onto the bed. And my jaw fell open. Amid the sheets of paper was a large leather hood. Two ears stood straight up, connecting to the base of the mask. A sharp, angular muzzle protruded from the front and a jaw hinged to the bottom. Along the back was a series of five buckles similar to the ones on my paws.

It was gorgeous.

"You like it pup?" Wagner asked.

I looked from him and back to the hood. It was the exact style I'd looked at, and I knew it wasn't cheap. Hell, none of the gear I was wearing was inexpensive. But as this final piece stared back at me, I slipped from the pup headspace and wrapped my arms around my wolf's shoulders.

"I love it."

Wagner's tail swung from side to side as he hugged me back. "Wanna try it on?"

That suggestion nudged me back in to headspace, and I sat back on my haunches, nodding with a soft ruff.

My wolf picked up the hood. I closed my eyes as the earthy scent filled my nose when he slipped it over my head. One by one, he clasped each buckle, tightening the hood to my face.

I finally opened my eyes: in the edges of my vision I could see the leather, but what stood out most was the muzzle protruding from my nose.

"This may be a bit loose, but I don't want to make it too snug. Want any tighter?"

I looked up at my wolf for a moment and rolled my neck. The leather wasn't quite pressed enough to my face. We took a moment to fine tune the tightness and we got the jaw moving a little more with my barks.

Waggy took a half step back. "That feel good?"

I let out a questioning call, and the noise rung in my ears. I wagged my tail with a happy series of barks. I set my paws to the edge of the bed and nuzzled again at his crotch.

"Hey, calm down." He took another step back. "We'll get there, but let's make sure the hood properly fits. Maybe we can play a little bit first?"

I gave a *whimper* of disappointment, but I knew he had a point. I began to wag my tail. Spinning in a circle, I pressed my chest against the mattress with my tail in the air.

"Good boy. Well, I found your rope. You want it?" He held up the rope bone, and I wagged harder. "Okay, go get it," he said as he threw it into the living room.

I slid from the bed and onto the floor and bounded after it. Again and again, I'd pick it up and bring it back. And each time, he checked again on the fit, tightening one strap at a time. As we played, Wagner moved us into the living room where he sat in a corner opposite the tree. And when the hood needed no more adjustments, I got an idea.

The jaw moved enough to where I could get one end or the bone rope in my muzzle. Tight enough to keep it there and play with, but not tight enough for a game of tug of war.

When I brought the bone back, instead of handing it to Waggy, I lifted my head and opened my jaw, sending the toy over his shoulder and landing behind him.

"Now why'd you do that, pup?" he asked. I sat back, wagging my tail.

Wagner shook his head. "You're a brat sometimes, you know that?"

I barked in agreement.

He scoffed as he rolled his hip, showing me his rear as he reached for the toy.

And that's when I pounced. With another bark of excitement, I jumped over him setting both my arms around his middle and pressed my hips to his and ground myself against his rear with a sexual growl.

"I guess that means you're done playing with toys, you sly dog?" Wagner asked looking over his shoulder.

I nodded, reaching a paw between his legs, feeling his growing length.

My wolf reached a paw back and rubbed my thigh. "I think

I can be talked into that. But we gotta clear off the bed first."

Without another word, I bounded off to the bedroom and jumped on the bed, scattering the box and papers from the mattress and around the room. When my wolf entered, I was on my back, arms up against my chest and knees bent with my legs spread. My shaft tented my jock, dampening it with pre.

"Someone's an eager pup," Wagner said, looking from my muzzle to my bulge and back. I attempted to wag in response, but I found it was harder to do on my back. Still, it made Waggy smile.

My wolf took off his shirt then unfastened his pants, letting them fall to the floor. My eyes traveled down his body. Wagner's gray fur was long, covering the definition of his muscles, but I knew the strength and power they held. My gaze wandered lower and saw the outline of his cock straining against his boxer briefs. He wasn't at full mast, but he was excited.

Waggy walked over to the bed, and I rolled over and out of the way, making space for him. He lay down beside me and rested his arm on mine.

"You're really enjoying yourself, aren't you?"

I let out a soft woof of agreement. Feeling my tail shift inside me and hearing the silicone thump beside the bed really made me happy.

What made me happier was when his paw began to trail down my side. Feeling his pads or claws run along my skin always gave me gooseflesh, and this time was no different. But when he moved to grab my rear, I pulled back.

My wolf tilted his head. "What's wrong?"

A small chuckle escaped me and I pounced him again. Wagner reached out his paws trying to stop me, but it was too late. I set my paws on his shoulders as I straddled him, grinding my bulge against his own.

"I think I understand. Not feeling like bottoming tonight?"

I shook my head.

"Okay. We can accommodate that." He set a paw between my legs, squeezing my cock through the fabric.

I let out a moan at the attention. He always knew how to get me going. Even with the slight differences between anatomies, there were enough similarities.

I slid back away from his attention and pressed my nose to his groin. The scent of his musk made me growl in desire. I pawed at his waist band, but my paws couldn't grab on.

"Let me help," he said, hooking his thumbs under the elastic and pulled them down. His shaft sprang up and connected to the side of my muzzle with a soft *thwap*. It wasn't my first time with his cock in my face, but it was with the added barrier. But I still wanted to try giving him some attention.

I placed my paws on either side of him and opened my muzzle wide. His tapered tip slid in easily, and the scent was stronger than ever before. With my muzzle around his cock, I pushed my head down. More and more of him slid forward, and when his tip finally found my lips, I ran my tongue along it, tasting him.

It was a wonderfully pungent flavor that was always uniquely Wagner. But with the concentrated scent in my muzzle, his taste was amplified as well. I couldn't help but start to wag and moan.

My wolf set his paws along either side of my head. "Pup, while it's hot seeing you enjoy yourself so much, your muzzle kinda hurts."

With another whimper, I pulled back and tried to focus on sliding the flat part of my leather paws along his length.

"That's a bit better," he said.

With a seductive ruff, I continued sliding my paws along his shaft.

"You don't have to do that, you know. You'll be pleasure enough."

I kept stroking him for another moment before crawling up the bed, closer to my wolf. I waited for him to meet my gaze, and once he did, I looked from him to the damp spot on my jock.

"You want some attention?" he asked.

I nodded and barked softly.

"Okay." He smiled up at me but instead of reaching for my shaft, he moved to the night stand.

I growled and tried to pull his paw to me.

Wagner turned back and tapped me on the nose. "Hey, give me that." He pointed a finger at me. "I don't like you going on dry, and I don't think you do either."

I huffed. He had a point. Lifting my paw from his, I gave a bark in apology.

"Good boy." Waggy reached back to the night stand and pulled out lube. "You gotta trust me to take care of you, okay?" Again, I nodded.

Shuffling a little closer, I sat up pup-style, exposing my prominent bulge to my wolf.

With the lube in one paw, he used the other to pull my shaft from the side of my pouch, pushing the fabric to the other side of my cock. Once I was exposed, he poured lube into his other paw and wrapped it around me.

I moaned as he slid along my sensitive flesh.

"How eager are you, pup?" he asked.

To answer, as he pulled back on my length, I pulled away from him, and when he slid forward, I did as well.

"I see." With a smile, Wagner continued along, letting me hump into his paw. "You wanna keep going here, or would you rather something warmer?" There was no other thought of what he meant.

And he didn't have to ask a second time. I pulled back, sliding my dick from his grip and started staring at his cock, wanting him to turn over so I could take his ass.

"You are an easy pup to please." Wagner hooked his thumbs under the elastic of his underwear and pulled them off his tail before sliding them fully down his legs. "You ready for this?" he asked as he got on all fours and spread his legs, shaking his hips from side to side. His tail swished, adding to the hypnotic effect.

I maneuvered between his legs and set my paws on his back. I felt my cock press against his rear and slide along his crack. As I humped against his backside, I started to growl in frustration.

"Want some help, pup?" Waggy asked.

I barked and nodded my head and a moment later, my wolf grabbed my length, pointing it in the right direction.

"Try there."

I pressed my hips forward, and this time his flesh let me in. Inch by inch, my cock was surrounded by his warmth. I pulled back and pressed forward again, filling him more. Back and forth, deeper each time until our hips met.

"Oh, baby, you feel so good." Wagner's tail tried to wag between us. Pressing my hips harder against him, I wagged my own.

"Come on, pup. Take what you wanted."

With that, I moved my paws around his hips and went to town. These short, deep thrusts pushed us close quickly—something we both liked and disliked.

"Oh, fuck." Wagner laid his head against the mattress while one paw worked his shaft. "Oh baby, I don't know how long I'll last."

As he bent over, I set my paws over the small of his back and gave my wolf longer, slower thrusts.

"Oh, come on, you tease. Don't make me wait."

I sped up again. Thrust by thrust, I could feel the onset of my climax, and I moaned.

"Get your release, pup. We both know you want it. And keep making those sexy noises."

With a growl, I picked up the pace. Moans mixed with growls and barks as I got closer and closer.

"Fuck, pup, that's so hot," Wagner said. The bed shook with not only the actions of my hips but that of his paw as well. And when he reached the other down to his cock, I knew he was almost there, teasing his knot.

"Ah, baby. I so close." He gave a long moan. "I'm coming."

A second later, I felt his muscles around my shaft contract, adding to the pleasure I already felt. And when the scent of the mess he made reached my nose, it pushed me over the edge.

With a howl-like moan, waves of pleasure pulsed through me as I filled my wolf. Each thrust deeper than the last, I filled him as much as I could.

And almost as quick as it started, the afterglow set it. I moved my paws back around Wagner's middle as I lay against him, nuzzling the top of his back.

"You enjoy that, pup?"

I barked out happy sounds. When I tried to wag, I let out a yip of surprise and pulled out.

Wagner looked over his shoulder, worried. "You okay?"

I coughed, nodding. "Yeah, just sensitive." I nodded to my now shrinking length.

"Want the gear off?"

I sighed. "Yes, please."

Piece by piece, the ritual was reversed. First my tail, then the mitts came off. With my hands freed, Wagner massaged them, working the feeling back into the muscles. Finally, clasp by clasp, Waggy removed the hood.

After the gear was off, he got up, ran to the kitchen and returned with a large glass of water and a washcloth. He made me drink before massaging my face with the cool cloth.

"You feeling good?" Wagner asked me.

I nodded behind the cloth. "Yeah. Kinda tired, but good. And a different tired from our usual sex."

"Gear might be warming you up. Maybe next time we try to lower the temp or add a fan."

I smiled. "That might be an idea. But for now, I just want to hold you."

Wagner chuckled. "I think we can do that."

The second week of our vacation was similar to the first. We skied, we relaxed, I pupped out, and we had sex. Both in and out of gear. We found the more we did the pup play, the less it was play, and the more it was cuddling and just being close. Sometimes, Waggy would be more dominant; other times, we'd be more on an even level.

Tonight, my eyes were on the clock. It was two minutes until midnight. Two minutes until the new year. And while we had been drinking white wine all evening, Wagner started pouring two glasses of champagne.

"Do we really need a different wine?" I asked

"Yes," he said, attempting to cork the bottle again. "I always have a single glass of stars at midnight."

I shook my head. "I'll chalk it up as another tradition of yours."

"Good." His tail wagged as he continued to prep.

A tablet showed a replay of Times Square hours before, and the ball dropped for real the first time.

"Okay, Wagner, last minute. Hurry up."

"Eat a piece of cheese and calm down. I'll be there in time."

I scoffed with a grin and did as he said. With thirty seconds left, he handed me a glass. We watched the lights in the square count down, and we joined in. Fifteen seconds.

Ten seconds.

Five seconds.

Three... Two... One.

"Happy new year," we both said. We touched our glasses, sipped our stars, and kissed. When we parted, my wolf had an extra spark in his eye.

"What are you planning now?" I asked.

"Nothing really. Just one last gift. I wasn't sure if I was going to give it or not, and decided I will." He walked back into the bedroom.

"You promise this is the last one? I feel bad with how much you've spent on me."

"I promise," he called. "And you shouldn't feel bad; I did all this because I wanted to, not because I had to."

I sighed. "If you say so."

A moment later he returned with a simple box.

Wagner handed it to me, tail wagging. "Go on, open it."

I did and inside was a thick length of leather folded in half. "What's this?"

My wolf smiled. "It's a collar. We both really enjoyed playing over the last two weeks, and I thought maybe we'd want this to be some kind of official thing. Not saying you have to, but... I mean..." His ears fell, and he took the box from my hands and fell to one knee.

"This isn't a proposal, but I want to continue to grow and learn with you. Will you take this and... and be my pup?"

"You sure this isn't a proposal? Feels a lot like it."

His gaze fell. "You're right. Maybe I'm being too dramatic with it." He started to get up.

I set a hand on his shoulder and pushed him back down. "You don't get out of this all that easily." I chuckled. "As long as I'm yours and you promise to care for me, I'll wear the collar."

Wagner's eyes lit up. "Of course baby. I'd be honored to."

I smiled. "Then in that case, Waggy, I'll add this to my gear collection and wear it with pride."

And like the nickname I gave him, his tail was going a mile a minute, and I began to copy him.

The Familiar

Linnea "Literalgrill" Capps

Katherine knocked on the door to Sarah Good's wattle and daub home, admiring the quality of the thatched roof in an attempt to distract herself from her growing nerves. Katherine had never understood how the feme sole had somehow managed to keep this home tucked away in the woods. Normally a man would dispute a woman 'owning' land to take it as his own, but somehow Sarah had managed to avoid such attention.

It was just another part of the air of mystery surrounding Sarah that only seemed to attract Katherine ever further to being overtaken by her wiles. She did not wish the dirt of unnatural lusts to contaminate the spring of her friendship with her, but there was no helping it. Her cravings were entirely contrary to the natural passions and desires she had been told were planted into nature by God, but they were there nonetheless. They could not be ignored.

Today, Katherine had determined that these emotions would finally be addressed. She had left her house, not telling her family of her plans for the day, as they would certainly not understand, so she could solve this problem. The devil be damned, she would no longer be swayed by temptation!

The door opened, Sarah's eyes sparkling as they realized who had come to her door.

"Katherine, my little kitty Kat! Please, do come in!"

Katherine's will to stand firm and remain outside melted away the instant Sarah's nickname for her was uttered. She could never understand why being compared to a mouser seemed to strike such a deep chord within her. Sarah's eyes, those bright blues like water running through a river, seemed to wash away Katherine's sense of propriety every time she witnessed them.

She sighed, already knowing she had been caught in the snare before she had even arrived. She had worn her finest petticoat, dyed with great expense to be the color black, that contrasted so powerfully with the white of her coif, shift, and apron. Katherine had told herself she wished to appear her finest to inspire her own confidence. In reality it had just been another effort to impress Sarah. The same as the jumbals she had packed for snacking upon in the basket she carried.

"Good morrow, Sarah. How do you fare today?" she replied all too merrily, unable to control her excitement as she entered the woman's home.

"Quite well! I had been hoping you might visit again today. I had even begun to prepare a syllabub for us to enjoy."

The foamy treat was quite fantastic to taste, with sugar, white wine, eggs, and of course cream whipped with frenzy. Katherine felt the heat creeping up under her skin. She knew how dearly mousers loved their cream. Sarah had delivered yet another barb designed to fluster her. No wonder she had these unnatural feelings with her friend constantly doing things like this!

She was determined to not show just how effective it had been, but her stutter betrayed her. "Y-Yes, that sounds lovely."

Katherine sat down at the table as Sarah returned to a small counter, grabbing bound birch twigs to whip up the delicious treat. The table was unnaturally precise in how it had been carved and built, certainly made with higher quality than even the local carpenter could provide. Katherine pondered where Sarah had gotten it; had she perhaps, somehow, made it herself?

She turned her gaze towards Sarah, admiring the elegant curve of her back beneath the draped fabric of her dress. She could see the gentle shake of her body as she whipped the syllabub, how the movement caused her earthy brown frock to sway, how it jiggled the curves underneath it. Katherine shook her head vigorously; what was wrong with her?

She had recently become eighteen years of age and knew she would soon need to find a man to marry. Her parents had said that the handsome Eli Bradford had come to enquire about the potential of bundling with Katherine for an evening. Even if it would help the family secure some rights to a wonderful water source off the Patomic River for the farm, she had found herself almost repulsed at the idea. Being tied from feet to waist in a heavy sack then sleeping next to Eli, who had suffered a similar fate, all in the name of "conversation", hadn't sounded pleasant to her in any way.

Yet, she might have considered it if somehow she could lay alongside Sarah. Perhaps the conversation itself could actually be pleasant, and the "conversation" after even more so. Drats, she was doing it again! She could never go on to do her duty towards her family if she allowed these lingering sinful thoughts to remain inside her mind any longer.

"Sarah, I must discuss something important with you."

Sarah was pouring the remaining white wine into wooden cups before carefully spooning the whipped topping above it to finish the layered drink. "Actually, if you do not mind, I, too, have something I must say. Might I go first?"

Sarah was taken aback, the small reserves of resolve she had tried to draw upon already draining away once more. "Why, of course, Sarah. What must you tell me?"

Sarah sat the cups of syllabub on the table, sitting herself across from Katherine. "I am tired of playing cat and mouse. Neither of us grow younger and it is beyond apparent the attraction you hold for me."

Katherine's jaw dropped, stunned into silence. How could Sarah be so frank about this? She had simply intended to say she could no longer visit her companion each day; Sarah just changed the game being played entirely.

"I c-couldn't fathom what you mean! We are friends, and such unnatural desires would be an affront to the Lord! How could you sugge—"

"Do you know of Sergius and Bacchus?"

Sarah had interrupted her again with a question that seemed

to come from nowhere. "Excuse me?"

"Sergius and Bacchus, two men that long ago achieved sainthood within the church."

Katherine kept silent, drawn in by Sarah's words. It was as though there was an unnatural force causing her to lean in, to listen further, as if some greater truth were about to be revealed. She had always felt drawn towards Sarah when she spoke, but this was different.

Sarah continued. "The two were brought together within the church. *Adelphopoiesis*, they called it; 'brother making'. Some would say it was truly a sign of their deep friendship. The truth of the matter is that the church was once not so strict upon its definitions of what was acceptable within the realm of love."

Katherine sat in silence, trying to contemplate Sarah's words. Was Sarah truly implying what she thought? Katherine could not have imagined that perhaps the lustful pangs within her heart were not purely temptations from the devil. Perhaps they were far more natural than she had ever known.

Sarah smiled knowingly, the look on her companion's face speaking volumes despite no words being said aloud. "Yes, my kitty Kat, I feel quite the same way as you do. I would be quite happy if you came to live in my home so that we might try spending our lives together."

Katherine wanted to throw all caution to the wind and embrace the joy bubbling up through her body. However, the reality of their situation had begun to crush her spirits like a stone.

"How could we? No one in Darlington would accept it. They would hang us, drown us, or something worse…"

"Oh, my little kitty Kat, you must have wondered how I have kept the menfolk of town away from my land all these years. I can keep you safe and by my side."

"It is true I have often wondered, but how could you manage such a feat as hiding us both? Certainly, my family would come looking for me."

Sarah had a mischievous look on her face as she stood, pulling a small length of cord hidden beneath her shift to reveal an iron key dangling from the end. She untied the cord, taking the key in hand while towards her kitchen, retrieving a thin box made of oak polished to a brilliant shine. She brought the box to the table, inserting the key and turning it before opening it so Katherine could see the contents inside.

"W-Wait, is that a wand?"

Katherine's eyes grew wide, Sarah taking the carved wooden implement from the box to hold with her left hand. "Yes, my kitty Kat, made from rare agarwood. It contains great power."

"Does that m-mean you are a w-w-witch?"

"Yes, my kitty Kat, but what you know of witchcraft is not all true. I am not bound by demons or some other such nonsense. I only learned magic so that I might live on my own, undisturbed by others. I have never found interest in men and did not wish to be hounded by them to become a wife my entire life. I had never expected to meet another who might feel the same."

Katherine wanted to turn and run. Perhaps if she went fast enough she could find her way to a priest and have the spell that Sarah must have cast upon her exorcised in some way. However, the idea of Sarah being pressed, those heavy stones placed upon a board crushing the gentle curves hidden below her dress, filled her with agony. Could she stand to remain miserable beside a man for the rest of her days knowing that she condemned the woman she had fallen for? That she had destroyed her one chance to find true happiness? That she would never feel awash in Sarah's blue eyes ever again?

The answer was no.

"How would you keep me protected?"

Sarah beamed in response, standing up once more to walk towards then lift the top off a chest next to her bed, rummaging through it. "Have you ever heard of a witch's familiar?"

Katherine frowned, trying to remain stern and not stare at Sarah's rear, framed delicately by her brown petticoat.

"Aren't those demons that take the form of animals to serve a witch?"

Sarah clucked, waving a hand dismissively in the air

dismissively. "I already told you there's no demons involved in any of this. Trust me, my kitty Kat."

Those two words, once again knocking down whatever walls Kathrine had tried to build up around her. Sarah took such control of the situation and Katherine could see the appeal of not needing to worry, to completely place her trust in Sarah. Still, that might be her last chance to turn back. Should she take it?

"Alright, I trust you. What is it I must do?"

Sarah returned to the table, whatever quarry she had retrieved from the chest concealed behind her back. She tapped the wand held in her left hand to the glasses of syllabub.

"First, we both drink up!"

Katherine eyed her companion in confusion. "Really? That's it?"

"I thought you said you trusted me! Now come, my little kitty Kat, and happily drink your cream."

Katherine's breath hitched, her cheeks glowing pink, but she dutifully complied. The cream truly was an utter delight, the richness of it coating her tongue. She wondered if syllabub had always been this good, but had no time to overthink it once the sweet wine began to mingle with the cream. She gulped down the entire drink in moments, already eying the other cup with an animalistic hunger.

"Please, help yourself, kitten."

She was too clouded with thoughts of more cream to object to yet another comparison of herself to a mouser and a tiny one at that. She gulped down the concoction, too engulfed in the pleasurable drink to notice the very object of her desire was disrobing before her.

"Sarah, that was delicious! What did you do to my dr—"

Katherine was stunned into silence; the body she had tried avoiding the temptations of imagining now laid bare before her. She had never realized just how long and luxurious Sarah's golden locks had been, always hidden modestly under a coif. The blonde lengths of hair hung down just past the delicate line of her collar bone. Sarah's body was plush, sporting soft curves and tantalizingly smooth skin.

She was far more gorgeous than any image Katherine's mind could have summoned. A thought occurred of how soft and marvelous Sarah's breasts must be, Kathrine thinking she wanted nothing more than to rest her head against them. Although if the prickling of her skin was anything to go by, she desperately wanted far more.

"Come, kitty Kat, let us lay in bed together."

A fire was sparking in Katherine's abdomen, the heat of it burning under her skin. She was beyond flustered, realizing during all the forbidden moments of fantasizing she had never actually thought of getting this far. She understood the basic mechanics of sex with a man. What would she do with another woman?

"W-What would you have me do Sarah?"

Sarah turned, strutting slowly towards the bed, each step and sway of her hips almost hypnotic to Katherine. "There is still some of the whipped cream in the bowl on the counter. Bring it to the bed. I know how kittens are with their cream, but be a good girl and don't drink any along the way okay?"

Katherine dutifully did as she was told, desperately fighting the temptation to take a finger full of it to taste. Her blood seemed to buzz within her body, too unnaturally to be purely from the paltry amount of wine she had consumed. Light-headed, she practically scampered towards Sarah in her eagerness to please.

"There's a good girl! Now, proper kittens need to look the part." Sarah took the bowl of delicious creamy goodness, setting it beside her on the bed. She untied Katherine's apron, tossing it aside on the floor. She then took what looked to be hemp rope, dyed black and woven to look as though it was a cat's tail, tying it around Katherine's waist. "On your knees, please, my kitty Kat."

Katherine complied, sinking slowly to her knees, her eyes darting between the nude form before her and the bowl she wanted to drink the contents of. Sarah removed Katherine's coif, letting the brown locks of hair hidden within tumble down her back, before placing what looked to be black cat's ears attached to a bent birch twig on Katherine's brow. Sarah reached behind her to grab her want in her left hand once more, tapping it on the bowl.

"Perfect. Now, my kitten…" Sarah set her wand down, taking the bowl and tilting it to drip some of the whipped treat down her chest, the sweet concoction coating her breasts. "You may have some cream."

Katherine clumsily lurched forward; there would be no more thoughts of the impropriety of it all. Having been given permission, she was no longer able to hold back a second longer. She caressed the soft mounds on Sarah's chest, licking heatedly at the cream. When she reached Sarah's nipples she latched upon them, swirling her tongue over the aroused peaks.

Sarah's breath hitched, body trembling in pleasure from the attention. "Good kitten…" She tried to gently move Katherine's head away, but she would not have it, keeping up her gentle kneading of those ample inviting curves.

"Kitten!" Sarah was more forceful this time, grabbing Katherine's hair and forcefully yanking her head away. The sting of it caused a jolt of electricity to shoot down her body towards her groin.

"S-Sorry, Sarah, I was just—"

Katherine swallowed hard. The rest of the syllabub cream was falling from the bowl. She watched with rapt attention, eyes following as the white indulgence teased its way down Sarah's body, dripped down past her navel, then down over her nethers. Katherine couldn't help but lick her lips.

"Be a good kitty Kat and clean that up, would you?"

Katherine accepted the invitation with gusto, tongue trailing around Sarah's navel to clean it. She once again noticed her blood was practically buzzing, as if static was crackling its way through her entire form, urging her towards the delicate folds further down on her lover's body. Katherine felt nerves creeping in. She tried to stall, licking some of the goodness that had made its way to Sarah's thighs. She had never even performed such an act, let alone considered doing something like this before. Was she sure about this?

Her moment of hesitation turned into uncontrollable craving, wanting nothing more than to taste the cream a mouser so craved, to please her owner, her master, her mistress? She *must* please her mistress!

It was as though this energy coursing through her body pressed at her head from behind. Katherine was no longer holding back, lapping away at the creamy goodness that glazed Sarah's folds. Her mistress's thighs were quivering, squeezing her thighs until Katherine felt slight pressure on the sides of her face. She placed her hands on those thighs, trying to hold those thighs apart, trying to delve her tongue deep into Sarah's entrance, determined to get every last bit of her treat and please her mistress.

Sarah raked her nails through Katherine's hair, once again taking it in a tight grasp to pull her kitten towards her. She moved her hips forward, grinding her slit headily against Katherine's lips, darkened with her juices. Katherine lapped away dutifully, in experience made up for with enthusiasm if Sarah's gasps and moans were any measure.

It was as though with each wave of pleasure crashing through her mistress was being transmitted by what Katherine realized must be magic into her own body. Her mistress's pleasure was her own; Katherine felt an animalistic need to bring them both to climax. She was drowning in pleasure as each wave grew larger, a stormy sea whipped into a sexual frenzy, the rope of an anchor stretched so tight it was about to snap.

"Good girl!" Sarah cried out, her back arching, each quake of her body in pleasure sending a rippling jiggle across her tender curves. Katherine could feel herself so close to reaching her own climax; if only she could pleasure her mistress further, maybe she could be pushed over the edge herself! She pressed against Sarah's clenching thighs with her paws...

Her paws? Katherine jolted back, her shriek of confusion sounding far more like a mewl as her ears pinned themselves against the side of her head. That sensation alone caused another wave of panic as she reached up for her head, feeling that the once cloth and birch "ears" she'd been wearing were now quite real and alive. Each tuft of black fur sprouting from her body caused a strange prickling on her skin. She tried to call out to Sarah in fear and confusion, but nothing but she could do nothing but meow.

Sarah was giggling as she watched the show. "Yes, kitty Kat?"

Katherine's vision was turning to shades of blue and green, the usual rainbow of the world far more muted than she was used to. Her dress began to grow loose, her entire body shrinking down to the size of a common mouser. She struggled to wiggle her way out of the fabric, walking out on all fours.

She could feel her fur rising, a hiss escaping her newly formed maw. Sarah picked her up by the scruff of her neck as though she had often practiced the movement.

"Oh, hush. It's not like you can't become somewhat human again! You're just thinking too much like a cat right now because the spell is fresh."

Sarah set the feline into the crook of her free arm, allowing her to nestle against her chest just how Katherine had wanted to earlier. A small rumble was starting to build up in her chest. Was she purring?

"See! There's a happy kitten!" Sarah scratched behind her ears, pleasurable tingles rocketing through the feline's form at the touch. "When you're near the people of Darlington you'll be like this, my black cat. The town will only remember the black stray that runs through town and nothing more. They won't come looking for you."

The idea that her family and friends could somehow forget her would have been frightening if she hadn't felt so overwhelmed from all of the petting. It was a joy unlike she had never been able to experience before, simply intoxicating. Her worries were dissolving around her; she was warm and safe in her mistress's arms. What more could she ever want? She barely cared when a collar with a small bell was placed upon her neck, and almost didn't catch Sarah explaining how it would help keep the spell in place.

Sarah was laying back in the bed, not taking time to clean up, pulling a blanket over both of their forms. "You'll be able to take a more human form again here at home with practice. That, or I could simply use my wand." She was giggling once more, seeing just how steady Katherine's breathing had become, feeling the rhythmic rumble of purring in her own chest.

"But I suppose all this can wait until tomorrow…"

It was quite odd getting used to having a tail. It seemed to either portray her every emotion against her will, or served as the perfect counterbalance as she tried to master walking on all fours. Even when returning to a more human form, the tail and her ears would remain, as well as the jet black fur that now covered her entire body. She hadn't been able to turn herself back yet as Sarah had suggested she might be able to. Her mistress needed to tap her gently with her wand to cause the transformation to take place.

She felt strangely naked upon her first time returning to her usual self. Soft skin replaced with fur still left her feeling exposed; she had looked to try and find her dress only to see Sarah smiling silkily with a giggle.

"Oh, kitty Kat, I sold your dress while you slept! No one else can see you this way, anyway, and you make for a far better view this way! Besides, good kittens have no need for clothes, right?"

With those words, Katherine came to accept that her new life in 'human' form would come with far less modesty than she had ever expected possible. Still, this came with its own perks. It seemed that Sarah's lustful cravings were almost impossible to satisfy and seeing her partner's nude form inspired her to act upon them often.

After being told that, "a familiar's job is to please their mistress", a phrase that had caused her entire body to feel warm despite her lack of clothes, she had set to work washing laundry. Her tail was thrashing in flustered embarrassment as she scrubbed down one of Sarah's frocks. She hadn't even heard that Sarah was sneaking up behind her, only learning this fact once she felt her hand shoved between her legs from behind.

Katherine mewled in surprise, making to drop the dress and

turn back but stopped in her tracks by Sarah's command.

"You will be a good kitten and continue washing while your mistress enjoys herself."

Katherine hadn't been sure what felt better as she desperately tried to keep focus, the splintering waves of pleasure as one hand caressed over the soft inner fur of her ear, or the other hand digging its fingers deep inside her delicate entrance. No matter her attempts at focus, Katherine was unable to hide just how powerfully her legs quivered as she rested her weight on her knees, nor her sounds of pleasure when she was plunged into climax.

Sarah simply got up as if nothing had happened, teasingly quipping, "You're acting awfully odd; is something wrong, my kitten? Come, finish your washing so it might hang to dry properly. We have much to do today!"

Katherine found that her mistress often liked to play many games this way, and found herself becoming lost in the fun of it all. She might be forced once more to maintain composure while managing simple household tasks or find dinner would need to be cooked with only one paw as Sarah demanded the other be dedicated to her pleasure at the time.

The only times such games did not seem to take place was during slumber, when she would curl her soft fuzzy self into a tight ball to rest upon her now favorite bed of her mistress's breasts, or when Sarah would need to venture into Darlington for food or supplies.

"Can't I come with you, Sar— my apologies. Mistress?" It was another game they had begun to play, Katherine finding submission treated her well. It simply felt right somewhere in the depths of her core to refer to her superior as mistress.

"Now, I know you could take your catlike form, my little kitten, but we can't risk you suddenly transforming in front of the townsfolk! So until you get a little more control I'll need you to stay home."

Katherine wanted to object, but Sarah tapped her wand on her pet's forehead, her body shrinking down to become a cat once more. With only a maw to speak from, she could do nothing but meow in protest.

"So please, stay home and practice! If you're a good girl, I'll even bring you home some cream. Would you like that, kitten?"

The feline knew just what her mistress was implying. The rumbling purr filled her chest before she could even think on the matter further.

"There's my good girl. Why don't you explore a while in your new body? It's quite fun to be a cat, you know!"

Summer turned to fall as the feline began to discover just how true this could be. How utterly relaxing it could be to rest in a windowsill, light from the sun pouring its warmth onto her furred form. She understood why mousers had that nickname, finding it exhilarating to chase any vermin that dared enter her mistress's home she must defend.

Winter came, the feline's body feeling all the more her own when warm fur fought away the cold tundra of the outside world. Roaring fires and resting on her owner's lap brought on the epitome of contentment within the cat. How could she ever want to ever leave her owner? Sure, she could entertain herself when mistress left the home, but things were far more fun when they spent time together.

Come spring, she stopped asking to go with mistress into town. Good kittens didn't need to follow their owners around in such ways! She could busy herself with chores, preparing herself to please her mistress upon her return. If there was time to spare, she could scamper around their home or the woods surrounding it, climbing trees and trying to catch the birds that would live within them. That or simply enjoy a comfortable nap on her favorite cushion.

She crept her midnight paws forward, ears telling her things no other sense could in the stillness. She heard the distinct sound of crisp vegetation snapping as her quarry, a quail she had been tracking for at least a mile, walked through the tall grass. Her tail thrashed carefully, left then right, as if trying to relieve some inner tension. Her back legs pedaled carefully, trying to find the perfect position to pounce while ignoring the aching of her old hips.

The quail must have been particularly aware or her collar's bell had given her away, bursting into flight before the cat could sink in her claws. As she flew away, the feline huffed in frustration. Mistress needed a new quill and she had hoped to be a good kitten and bring home both feathers and dinner at once to solve the problem. Still, the day did not need to be lost. Mistress always chastised her for bothering any neighboring farms, but at times the punishments for disobeying were not entirely unpleasurable.

She gambled today might be one of those times. She could simply steal a chicken from a farmer! Sure, chicken feathers weren't quite so fine as quail, but they were perfectly serviceable. Plus, having brought home dinner, certainly mistress wouldn't be too harsh if she fried it in oil with breading just how she liked it!

She made her way out of the tall grass, padding her way down an oddly familiar path as she pondered just how fortunate she truly was. Her owner had been so kind to bring her inside and offer her the chance to serve as a familiar so she wouldn't have to live out in the elements any longer. Then she had bestowed upon her the honor of being a familiar and the ability to take human form! She couldn't remember much of her former time as a stray in the wilds, but she could not recall any other animal having shapeshifting abilities as she had. She was truly the most blessed of all felines, able to fulfil her sole purpose of bringing joy in any form she could to mistress.

Kitten, or at least that's what her owner had named her, arrived on the farm. She eyed the house, knowing she needed to avoid whatever humans lived inside. She knew six lived on this property at least. Wait, how did she know that? No matter; it was information that could be quite useful.

She stalked toward the house, keeping low to the ground in hopes she wouldn't be seen. This dark fur of hers could be such a bother when not hunting at night. However, most tended to avoid her out of superstition. No one wanted to cross a black cat's path, and that privacy could be enjoyable at times such as these.

She found herself quite startled to find there were far more children running around the house than she had expected. Was there an event taking place here of some kind? She sat herself down behind a tree, considering it might be best to give up and turn home. Then she heard the gentle sobs of a human being held close by another. She stalked her way towards the sound, her catty curiosity too much to ignore.

The two embracing seemed quite old, even by human standards, the two having graying hairs upon their heads. The female was the one who was sobbing, the man with her offering gentle encouragement.

"I know this always brings you great sadness, Annabel, but we must not show it to the grandchildren. Not when such a miracle takes place inside."

"I know, Edmund, it just is so difficult. I had always imagined she would be the one to bear grandchildren with Eli. Seeing our young Christine having her third just brings such emotions upon my soul."

Kitten felt a faint buzzing at the back of her skull. Why were these names so familiar? The sensation grew stronger the longer she tried to think about it until it became too overwhelming to be considered any longer. She dismissed the thoughts from her mind with a shake of her head. These humans were obviously bothering her in some way; she should make her way past them and towards the chickens. Perhaps she could still capture one while they were distracted by whomever was giving birth.

Still, as she successfully snuck past she couldn't help but feel a faint sense of unease. She knew the land all too well, each tree and hiding spot, as though she had been there before. She could not remember such a time, nor even how she had known the farm was there in the first place. Her tail twitched in annoyance. What was happening today?

The buzzing inside of her mind became like that of bees within a hive, causing her to cry out in pain. She did her best to drown out the thoughts, focusing only on her greatest comfort, her mistress. How she would be so proud of Kitten bringing home dinner to cook, how she could prepare several feathers as quills, how mistress might grant her the opportunity to lick between her thighs and over her pleasure as thanks. She was about to continue walking, now calm, when the sudden slamming open of a door caused her to jump in alarm.

"It's a girl!" a voice shouted so all who were outside could hear. "She'll be named Katherine!"

Her ears perked, hearing the older woman sobbing once more. "So sweet of her; so kind to honor our dear Katherine who vanished so long ago."

It was as though her heart became ice, her entire body growing cold. Her body trembled, flooded with an anxiety stronger than any she had ever known. She could not stay there a moment longer. She raced to the chickens while she could, killing one with ease before dragging it by the neck to scamper hurriedly home. She only made one stop along the way to pick a small twig with berries. She wanted to be sure to make a meal that her mistress could never forget.

"Did you enjoy your chicken, Sarah?"

Sarah was awaking from her slumber. A sickly sweet taste seemed to be coating her tongue. She was confused, having not heard her familiar use that name for years. In fact, when had she even fallen asleep? She attempted to rise from the bed but found her arms and legs were bound to the sides of it with hempen rope.

"Kitten! What is happening?" Sarah's voice rang out with confusion. She turned her head, seeing a fire that burned far too large for summertime, the tips of her two pronged fireplace poker glowing red as it rested on the blazing logs.

"How many years? How many years did you steal from me?"

"K-Kitten?" Sarah was downright alarmed now, looking to the far corner of the house to see her familiar looming there, dressless as always, but with anger gleaming in her eyes.

"Katherine! You will call me Katherine! How many years did you steal from me?"

Sarah swallowed hard. Her spells hadn't been strong enough;

somehow her familiar had remembered. Still, she hadn't become a witch by having no wit; she could talk her way out of that situation. If she could find a way to get her hand on her wand...

"Thinking about this?" Katherine pulled the wand out from behind her back, mockingly holding it in her left hand, a scene eerily reminiscent of one that had taken place years ago. "Don't bother; it won't be of any use once it becomes ashes."

"Kitten, wait!" But there was no stopping her; Katherine flung the wand into the fire. It barely lasted a moment, whatever magic contained inside bursting out as the wand quickly burned away into nothing.

"Katherine! My name is Katherine, and I trusted you. I trusted we would share our lives together, trusted you would keep me safe!"

Sarah had never known such fear. She was tied up and defenseless, with no magical escape possible. All at the mercy of the woman she had tricked into being enslaved to do her bidding for all these years.

"Darling Katherine, I *did* keep you safe! We've spent so much time toge—"

"At what cost? You stole everything from me! I have nieces and nephews; my parents have grown to an old age. I have known nothing of them! They wouldn't even have me now that I look like this..." Katherine was stalking towards the fireplace, taking the cool end of the poker in her hand before lifting the entirety of it from the flames.

"Patience, Katherine. I could make another wand. I could turn you back!"

It was obvious from the fear in her voice just how desperate Sarah had become. Her eyes were wide, those sparkling blues flooding with terror at the red hot poker in the hands of her once pet. It was apparent what she planned to do.

"Patience? Perhaps I have not lost so much of my life that I cannot manage patience. Tell me, Sarah. How many years have you stolen from me?"

Sarah squirmed against her bonds helplessly. Her only hope now was honesty. Maybe the woman who once loved her so dearly would have mercy. Especially if she could manage a good excuse.

"Eight years… I am so sorry, Katherine. Please, forgive me…"

Katherine sobbed desperately at the answer. No wonder her hips had always felt so sore; as a cat she would be over 26! Incredibly old for such a species, but the perfect marrying age as a human. Not that she ever could now. Any hopes at finding happiness had been stolen from her. She continued approaching with the flaming hot poker, brandishing the two pronged device menacingly.

"I never meant to become a witch, to use such a spell. Satan used his powers of temptation against me! I was forced to ensorcel you as part of his horrendous scheming."

Katherine laughed maniacally. Sarah knew she had misplayed.

"Liar! 'Not bound by demons or some other such nonsense' were your exact words, weren't they?"

Sarah could not think of a response, her breath growing ragged and rapid in fear, the poker edging ever closer to her flesh.

"I may never know the joys of my family. I may never know the tender embrace of the angels upon entering heaven when I die. I may have to know the taste of flames in the pits of hell when I pass. But you, my 'mistress', will never know joy again. You, Sarah, shall experience just how hot flames can burn in your time here on earth."

Katherine took aim, and before Sarah could cry out once more begging for mercy, impaled both prongs into the two most tender entrances of her body. She screamed in agony, the most sensitive nerves of her body being tortured beyond all reason. A sickening sizzle filled the air as she choked and sobbed. By the time Katherine pulled out the pokers, the acrid scent of burnt flesh hung in the air.

Sarah's body quaked, quickly racing towards a state of shock but not reaching it quite yet. Katherine let the poker fall to the ground, the sound of iron clattering loudly.

"My goodness, my apologies, *mistress!*" Sarah said, her voice dripping with sadistic levels of sarcasm. "It seems you have burned yourself! Something to aid in healing... Oh, I know!"

She walked towards a kitchen counter, grabbing a small container of seal salt sitting upon it. Sarah's eyes practically bulged from their sockets. Yes, it could aid in healing, but the pain at how much it stung would be even more horrific than what she knew now.

"Please, Katherine! I'll do anything, anything you wish. Anything but that please dear God please!"

Katherine pondered it for a moment before striding towards her. "Very well, perhaps I have a use for a servant just as you did." She straddled Sarah's chest, glaring down at her. "I suppose if you keep me happy, you could potentially keep yourself from further pain. Maybe I'll even keep you alive."

Sarah had no choice. What else could she do? At least this stalled for time, gave her potential for a future escape. She opened her mouth, her tongue slowly coming out to lick at Katherine's nethers, before Katherine thrust herself forward. She sat down with all of her weight on Sarah's face, covering her mouth and nostrils so she couldn't breathe.

"Come on, "pet"! Get to work!"

Sarah did her best to comply, parting the soft folds with her tongue, swirling and fluttering it around inside. Katherine gave no reaction, looking entirely unimpressed.

"You really don't value breathing all that much, do you, Sarah?" Katherine reached behind her to grab one of Sarah's nipples, twisting it far too hard to be anything but painful.

Sarah squealed, a majority of what little precious stores of breath were still contained within her lungs being lost. She writhed her tongue furiously inside the velvety flesh as if her life depended on it, because she knew it quite literally did.

Katherine was finally starting to show signs of emotion, panting slightly. Sarah's lungs now felt as though they were burning, but she continued onward, desperately hoping she could please her captor. She needed air; she needed to breathe! Her entire body was writhing, fighting against her bonds as she struggled against what she thought must surely be her final moments before suffocation.

Katherine shivered, pulling away as her legs trembled. Sarah desperately gasped for breath, choking and coughing as it harshly entered her lungs once more.

"Not bad... Perhaps you will do even better with practice."

Katherine got off the bed, grabbing the container of salt before mercilessly dumping it upon Sarah's nethers.

As Sarah wailed in anguish, Katherine spoke in a commanding tone. "We can't have you dying, now, can we? Don't worry, 'mistress', I'll keep feeding you each day, keep you safe and healthy. Keep you away from the world. Maybe eventually, once I feel satisfied, I'll untie you from this bed."

Sarah could barely comprehend what was being said, the pain of it all far too much for her to pay attention to anything but how horrifically her intimates stung.

"But I suppose all this can wait until tomorrow..."

Katherine removed the collar from her neck, placing it upon Sarah's. She then made her way out of the front door before becoming a cat once more. She began to scamper away, the sound of a little bell ringing out in the night, the tinkling of its bright tones clashing against the blood curdling cries as her once mistress struggled.

She intended to make a brief midnight visit to the tailor in town. Perhaps she could come up with something quite creative to use some of the needles kept there for tomorrow. A fun game for her and Sarah to play. One of many that were to be played in the many months to come.

Deference of
Shining Joy

AI Song

I never really hit up bars and clubs, especially on Mondays, but with my viola in my paw I could be standing under a burning firmament raining hellfire on me and feel like I was just on a stage shrouded within a sparkling spotlight. Dog Haus was definitely a new environment to practice in. Bavarian memorabilia lined the dark, wooden walls. A sizeable stage overtook the east end of the bar, flanked by many cushioned booths. A fairly large bar near the entrance was lined with bright, neon lights, yet they never lit up the entire space of the leather club.

I hammered my bow against the strings to accent the last few notes of *Viola Sonata in D Minor* by Glinka as the rest of the quartet cheered. It was great that we finally got through it with only minor issues. The wallaby on the cello was able to find a friend to turn the piano accompaniment into parts for a cello and two violins, though he kept averting his gaze from me. The burly coyote on first violin ran through a game plan for next week's practice session while also telling each of us what we could improve upon and what we did well. He wore a smart dress shirt while the wallaby next to me was in dark, red flannel atop a retro, metal t-shirt.

"Hon, that was amazing," Lane said as he wrapped his thick,

pink rat tail around me, squeezing me tightly. His muscles threatened to wreck my frame, and he finally let go when I started coughing. "Sorry, cutie. We can only dream of getting to your level one day."

"It was nothing," I said and shrugged. "You guys did awesome too."

"You're too precious and modest, sweet Dhole," the buff rat said and kissed my cheek.

As I placed my viola, shoulder rest, and bow in their case I saw the others taking off their shirts and unzipping their pants. My rat tossed off his highlighter yellow hat, along with his neon shirt and hoodie to reveal his incredible abs and pecs. Dog Haus was closed on Monday nights and they were letting us use it as a practice space for our quartet, since they wanted us to perform at their next couple pup nights, and if we did well they might keep us on. Ezra, the bulky coyote, slipped on a green harness and pleather hat; he had helped with all the bookkeeping and the financial end to help start the leather bar up. Since I worked in downtown Seattle it gave me a chance to let the horrific weekday traffic dissipate before heading to north Seattle.

The coyote slipped on a large pair of shiny boots with lime green soles as the rat and wallaby were donning their pup masks; yellow and red, respectively. Ezra's harness and pleather cap had a streak of green running through them. He removed his khakis to reveal a dark, emerald jockstrap, which he removed and threw at Lane. The big rat took it and huffed it before taking off his gold briefs and getting on all fours.

After Bill took off his tattered, black jeans I noticed that he had been going commando this whole time. The chubby wallaby got on all fours and took the jockstrap in his muzzle, but the rat bit the other end and they tugged at it.

"Apollo! Sparky! Stop fighting!" the coyote commanded as he smacked each of their rumps harshly. They both whimpered as he shouted at the wallaby. "This is for the alpha! Not the whelp!" He then grabbed for the jockstrap and shoved it onto Lane's muzzle as Bill cowered with his head under one of the chairs. Our handler started petting and stroking Lane's upper back as he put the yellow collar around the rat's neck and clipped the faded pleather leash to it.

"C'mere, little pup," Ezra growled as he yanked on the chubby wallaby's large tail, who then lurched forward, knocking the chair off the stage.

"Bad pup!" he shouted, pulled out a *Searchlight* magazine from his briefcase, rolled it up, and then proceeded to smack Bill's ass again. He then wrestled the wallaby into submission and put him in a headlock before strapping the cherry red collar around his brown furred neck.

"It looks like one of my pups is missing. He's gonna get punished if he doesn't show up soon," the stocky coyote growled as he turned to me and shot me a threatening leer. From this I could've sworn I saw a glob of pre drip from his pointed tip. It was just the conical end that poked out from his sheath, and his large balls almost swung with each step he took towards me.

I felt my breath hastening due to this incredible scene happening before me, but also because I wasn't sure if I could measure up. Bill and Ezra had bellies like me, but Ezra had such muscular arms and legs, and Bill was cute and proportional. I was just fat. Lane was a bodybuilder in training, and I never understood why anyone like him would like someone like me.

I took off my indigo golf shirt and the turquoise sweater vest, clinging to it along with my jeans and briefs. I then slipped on my blue and black hood and proceeded to get on all fours. The mask covered my head in a nice, snug manner, but the mandible was missing, so I could suck dick at the drop of a leash. It was a birthday gift from Lane, who introduced me to this new world.

"It looks like we've got a stray on our paws here," Ezra said in his sultry, yet demeaning tone as I felt my pointed tip slowly slip out from my sheath along with the chemical burn of the acid churning in my stomach.

So far I'd only had sex with Lane, and I practiced with the other two a couple times before. When Lane suggested we have some fun with his other two boyfriends I agreed because I wanted to please him, and I was curious about the others. Bill had a nice pair of fat cheeks, and Ezra was certainly daddy material, but it was just all so intimidating. My heart was racing due to both excitement and anxiety. Why had I thought I was ready for this?

"Get over here, new pup." His rich, baritone voice boomed, and I crawled over slowly. The meekness was intended to be an act for him, but I really was feeling shaky and unsure. "What should we name you?"

The coyote got down on one knee and began inspecting me. He then placed a large paw on my flank then moved it down to my belly and began rubbing it in slow circles. As he massaged my stomach I tried to take slow breaths, but I ended up taking shallow ones and then forgetting to breathe.

Despite the discussions about engaging in the pup play scene together, I was still feeling uncertain about all of this. I had agreed to what Ezra, Lane, and Bill offered, but in the moment I was feeling off.

He placed a paw on my russet rump and lifted my tail as I gently quivered and felt my cock jump. He spread my cheeks and chuckled as he worked his way down fondling my balls. My knot started swelling in my sheath, and he grabbed my shaft and yanked it out as I yipped.

"You've got a patch of white on your rump, hmm," he said smirking down at me. He then grabbed my cheek and my tail faltered curling between my legs, as my boner dripped a long strand of pre onto the wooden stage.

"Let's call you…Spot." His finger traced a circle on my ass and suddenly his palm was on the back of my head shoving it into his throbbing package. The smell of his desire and the musk from his groin was intoxicating, yet the butterflies in my stomach were furiously transmuting themselves into a storm of locusts desiring to tear me apart from the inside out.

My knot then swelled further as I witnessed the other two were sniffing one another and wrestling, with Lane finally atop the chubby wallaby. They then turned to me and stared.

Group sex was on my bucket-list, so why was I feeling this way? Half of me told myself to shut up and dive into this pristine, cerulean pool of sex, and the other told me to run home and never talk to another soul again.

"You like that, stud?" he whispered in my ear. "You're gonna breed…that red pup's rump, and make a new litter for daddy, okay?"

I just whimpered in response.

"You need to be more enthusiastic than that, Spot. Your cock's dripping, Spotty boy. Why isn't your enthusiasm matching? I thought you'd be happy in this home," under the dim bar lights that somehow felt brighter and hotter than before.

The other two crawled over to me. Bill was growling as Lane giddily hopped over and jumped on me. This was supposed to be sexy. This was supposed to be what I wanted. This was the dream for so many guys out there. So why did my heart feel like it was going to stop, and why was my stomach so queasy, and why was I breathing so fast, and why did it feel like the atmosphere was on fire even though I was naked?

"Lava lamp," I whimpered the safe word and gasped for air.

Ezra put his paws up and said, "Everything okay, Dhole?"

"You alright, Kyle?" the rat asked.

"I just, I… I need to go to the bathroom," and I stood up and immediately walked to the bathroom. The neon strands of light along with the smell of booze and sex mixed in my mind as a synesthetic wave of chaos and confusion washed over me. I ran into the rustic wooden door face first, and realized I needed to turn the handle.

I huffed and held myself as I made my way into the small space and flicked the light switch. Blue. The calm light was the inverse of the bar lighting; it was dim, yet it flooded the entire room. It was a little alienating, but the turquoise was also sort of soothing. I was also glad they cleaned up the single stall bathrooms before they closed. I turned the lock, placed a toilet liner sheet on the seat, and sat down with my head in my paws. I took off the mask, placed it next to the sink, and looked up to see a framed photo of a fox in a leather jacket with nothing else on. Behind him was a half-timbered house with a string of lights across it. The fox himself had some pretty large balls and was peeking from his sheath. I wanted to see his knot.

My mind focused on the handsome fox, and I thought about being alone with him in this bathroom, safe and comfortable in his arms.

"Kyle, you okay in there?" I heard after a few soft knocks.

"Yeah, I'm fine," I said quickly.

"Can I come in?" Lane asked.

I unlocked the door and sat back down as the gray rat entered while removing his hood and shut the door behind him gently.

"Hey, bud. You doing alright?"

"A little," I said, turning up to look at him bathed in the cool, sapphire light.

"Do you need a hug?" He opened his arms wide for me.

I nodded and nuzzled his muscled chest as I felt his strength wrap around me. I took in his masculine musk as I placed my nose between his pecs. Eventually I turned around and reclined on him.

What I loved about Lane wasn't just his looks or his muscles, but his attitude towards life. He was always so happy and sweet, despite working in IT at the University of the Pacific Northwest. Whenever my coworkers or boss or random callers got upset with me I never took it well. Usually I would sulk for the rest of the day, but when bad things happened to him, somehow he was always able to work through it.

His workplace was my alma mater where I studied music performance, but they never gave me an interview, and I still felt aimless career-wise, unless an orchestra wanted to take me on. At least working as an administrative assistant at Zenith Solar Panel Services was a somewhat comfortable job.

My roommate worked with Lane and told him about me. I kept telling the buck about all the auditions that never went through along with all the interviews I bombed. One day Lane popped over as I was practicing. He told me he and his boyfriends were trying to start up a string quartet and needed a new viola player. I was playing *Csárdás* by Vittorio Monti, since I had completely failed at an audition and wanted to wallow. The rat busted into the apartment and asked me to play something impressive. I ran through Paganini's twenty-fourth caprice and he asked me if I wanted to complete the quartet.

The two of us loved going to indie concerts and with him holding me from behind as we watched and swayed to musicians bathed in golden lights.

As the happy memories flooded my mind the buff rat kissed me. In some ways things were simpler like that, and I just wanted everything to be easy and understandable and calm.

"I'm here for you, hon," he whispered gently in my ear as he rubbed my belly. "You're safe and sound."

"Thanks, Lane," I said and turned to give him a quick kiss.

"Of course," he said and patted my rump. "Should we get out of here?"

"I think I need a little time." I then kissed him back tenderly.

Lane opened his muzzle, and I slipped my tongue in. I then opened my own further, and he lapped at the entry. My length was slowly emerging from my sheath as I remembered the times when the rat was there for me when I got scared or sad. My thoughts shifted to the times when we made love and when I opened up my birthday gift from him and saw my blue pup mask for the first time. He was my big, strong alpha and he reamed me so hard that night.

I moved my paw down to his thick cock and began massaging it and playing with his large, shapely balls. It made me smile to know that he was getting so hard so quickly. I then got onto my knees and pulled back his foreskin, that engorged tip glistening in the cool, turquoise lighting.

The rat was a few years older than me, but most people who knew him always said he had the energy and attitude of a twenty-one year old. The fact that he was up for sex so much only made my days so much brighter.

I took his thickness into my muzzle and swirled my tongue around his engorged glans as he spurted pre into my muzzle. I worked his hefty balls as he twitched against my palate.

"Oh, hon, that's as good as fucking gold. Mm, you're the best, you sweet, little Dhole," he moaned.

I then hummed in response, which elicited more pleasurable sounds from the big rat. I massaged each nut with each paw and then began pumping his shaft while sucking the tip.

He moaned and groaned as I kept up my ministrations, and after a while he said, "Oh, hon, I'm gonna nut if you don't stop."

This only made me suck and bob faster. I teased that sensitive tip with my lips and tongue with more ferocity, and I tasted his salted pre, guzzling it down as he spurted it into me.

His breathing hastened as he bucked into me, yelling, "Fuck, hon, I'm gonna…" and then filling my muzzle with his delicious essence as he rubbed the back of my head and thrusted into my muzzle.

I stood up with my own cock bobbing at his face. I spit his load onto my palm and coated my cock. He slipped on his yellow pup hood and got on all fours.

"I know what you want, cutie," he said, then I wore my blue pup hood and followed suit. The rat lifted his large, pink tail and spread one of his cheeks for me.

"Any actual lube?" I asked, slipping on my own mask.

"If you didn't notice, I was wearing a butt plug for Ezra, but I took it out after you, uh, skedaddled," he said as I coated my throbbing cock in his essence. "We'll be okay."

I aimed my cock at his shiny pucker flanked by those amazing muscled cheeks. My conical tip rested at his warm entrance as I opened those slabs of muscle. Looking up at the fox on the wall, I fantasized about him joining us, letting me suck him off as I plowed my muscle rat.

Why was I even thinking about that? I could've been doing that just a couple minutes ago. Maybe it was because Ezra and Bill were actually there, and the fox was just someone I could make things up about. The guy in the frame wasn't judging me, nor could he say anything to hurt me.

In this bathroom it was just us. There was no one to make me feel bad about my performance. I pushed myself up to the knot into my boyfriend and pulled back out and received a delicious grunt from him.

"Hon, oh, I wish I could be holding your leash right now," he said with a low growl. "You deserved a yank for that."

"To punish me or to thank me?" I asked.

"Yes," he said coyly.

I then kept up my thrusts as he relaxed his hole and got down on his massive forearms.

"Keep it up, or there will be a punishment, little Dhole."

"Yessir," I replied.

"Dogs...don't talk," he chided, and I whimpered at him.

I kept thrusting as I felt the pleasure surge through my body at the incredible feeling of his warmth surrounding me. After a bit I was getting to my ceiling, and I soon kept slamming my knot against his entrance. I heard him grunt and snarl as I pushed it further and further into him, and soon with one final crescendoing scream it popped back in. I howled as I filled my boyfriend with my own pearlescent love. I then stepped over him and we were ass to ass.

"How are you feeling, hon?" he asked with exhaustion in his voice.

"Pretty good," I said, slouching. "I wasn't sure if I'd actually get off tonight. Thanks for checking up with me."

"Of course," he replied. "That's what boyfriends are for. So... Did you want to talk about what happened out there?"

"It's a couple things. I guess." I sighed.

"Alright," he said and squeezed me behind me knot.

"I don't know," I said after a grunt. "I guess I still feel like they're strangers to me despite practicing with them so much."

"I get that. I could be in class with someone five times a week, but still not really know them," he said with a softer tone. "Until I actually hung out with someone outside of class or work I guess they weren't really under my radar."

"Would they actually want to hang out with me?" I asked.

"Of course! I know Bill's been acting kinda unfair to you, but you guys are really into Anime and old Hollywood films. Both you and Ezra are super smart."

"I don't know if I'm that smart," I said and fiddled with my fingers.

"Stop it; of course you are. You guys could do an escape room together or visit a museum. You love things like that."

"Okay, that could be a lot of fun."

"I could try to turn his bedroom into an escape room. You have to put a dildo in a sex doll's ass and then the bathroom door opens or something like that! Yeah!"

I just shook my head and said, "Lane?"

"Yeah."

"You're the light of my life."

Ezra answered the door as I swiped through the Howlu app on his phone.

"Is there anything you'd prefer to watch?" I asked, scrolling down the comedy section with the bright chartreuse background.

"I'm good with basically anything," he said, handing over a few crisp, green bills to the kangaroo. The paper bags he held had read 'Yasaikana' and had a logo with green leaves in the shape of a school of fish. He also had a bag with two large, colorful drinks.

"One Midori Meal and a soy matcha latte boba for you," he said, putting the tall drink and sushi in front of me. The coyote bought a Tofu Platter and a kiwi green tea with aiyu jelly. The large canine sidled up to me, and I rested my head against his shoulder and nuzzled him.

Earlier that morning we had done two escape rooms and completed them both with ample time, and then we walked through the Japanese gardens. We definitely didn't want to give up a sunny spring day in Seattle to just being indoors all day.

After all the excitement we had wanted to have a chill afternoon, in multiple senses of the word. We had tried going through a few quick violin and viola duets with one another for about an hour. I opened my container and salivated at the sight of all the vegetarian sushi before me. I had rolls with avocado and cucumber and a number of amazing veggies, while Ezra's was filled with inari, a little container of vegan agedashi tofu, and some fresh and fried tofu rolls.

I kept looking through the LGBTQ+ section and tried to find something neither of us had seen and were in the mood for. We decided on *Lights, Camera, Attraction*, which was about two gay actors trying to make it in Hollywood. It had its schmaltzy moments, but was done really well.

We dug into our meal as we cuddled together. The handsome coyote popped a piece of inari into my muzzle as I had him try my matcha drink.

"I can see why you like sucking balls, Dhole," he said coyly, and we laughed harder than we probably should have. "May I put my paw on your leg?"

"Yeah, of course. I'd really like that," I said as he gently squeezed my thigh. I felt a stirring in my sheath, and I nuzzled him, taking in his rich, woodsy scent.

The rat and the wallaby were in Portland for the weekend, attending an EDM festival, so the two of us had the apartment to ourselves.

As the credits rolled we noticed the sun was setting, bathing the world around us in a gentle glow. Ezra turned on a few lights as my tail curled around me, and I looked down at my knees in my faded blue jeans. The coyote sat back down next to me.

"Are you doing okay?" he asked, keeping a cushion space away from me.

"Yeah. I don't know why I have to feel this way."

"It's okay. We don't have to," the older coyote said, gently.

"I want to. You're really handsome and you're so sweet to me."

"I feel the same about you, cutie."

"It's like…" I sighed. "I know you like me, but it took me a while to even have sex with Lane. Even though our date has gone really well and you're telling me that you find me attractive. I just feel self-conscious."

"I can relate," he said. "I'm not the skinniest guy in the world, and I've had a lot of guys tell me that they don't want a fat, old guy."

"Seriously? But you're so hot."

"It seems like a lot of guys want someone thin or muscular, and I don't fit that mold."

"I don't either."

"But I think you're adorable," he said. "And I really like you, Dhole."

"I like you too. To be honest, I'm already getting a boner."

"I have an idea. Let's get your viola out."

"You want to practice some more?" I asked.

"No, but you seem to be at your most confident when you're performing," he said. "We're gonna be half naked when we perform, so I want you to be able to handle that."

"I think I will be. Maybe. I mean, I've been playing viola since I was like ten," I said, opening the case, tightening my bow, attaching the shoulder rest and playing a few scales. "It's second nature to me now."

"What's something you enjoy performing, and that you've memorized like the back of your paw?" the coyote asked as he held me from behind.

I closed my eyes and began playing the first few bars of 'Passionate Confession' by Tchaikovsky. I performed it during my sophomore year of college as an exam piece. One thing the general public didn't seem to know was that Tchaikovsky was gay, so I had channeled all the pain of what he probably went through as I performed the piece, all the fear and uncertainty.

This time I focused more on the passion than the confession. Maybe this time that Russian fox had met someone else who was gay in his early twenties and he wanted to show how much he liked the other guy. This time I wanted a brighter and more relaxed tone. I also wanted the color changes to reflect something closer to the sunset.

I felt the coyote wrap his arms around my waist more tightly as I felt myself almost leaning against him. I was also thankful he knew how to position himself so that he wouldn't be in the way of my bowing arm or mess up my neck posture.

Soon his stiffness was against my rump as I gently grinded against it.

As I bowed, I let the strings sing out for a bit longer as I accented a few of the shorter notes and let my creativity flow through the soundboard. I let the final notes cry out and then dissipate as the sun disappeared over the buildings across the street.

"That was incredible," he said and kissed me on my neck.

"Your skills are flawless."

"I wouldn't say I'm perfect."

"Just take the compliment, Dhole. This is your life and passion."

"I do love it," I said. "Fifteen years… and I barely have a career with it. How did you get into violin?"

"Just like you, I started in middle school, and I fell in love with it. Orchestra was the only class that I really looked forward going to. Then high school hit, and I found that I couldn't practice as much as I wanted to."

"I know that feeling." I nodded.

"Well, I studied finance and music, but I had to divide my time in half between the two," he said, turning to the sky, which was fading from orange into a dark indigo, "and then I chose the path of money and a stable life rather than pursuing music."

"You probably made a good choice doing that."

"Well, I just feel like I'm making rich people even richer, and I'd rather be doing something creative or helping those with less or marginalized people like us."

"I guess everything's a tradeoff when it comes to time," I said and placed my viola back in its case along with its accoutrements. "So, I do want to spend it wisely."

The coyote placed a paw onto my lower back as I put mine on his chest. Our muzzles then met, and I felt warmth spread across my face. Our tongues then began lapping one another's as I began to unbutton his shirt. He then began removing my blue cardigan and I ended up with my back on the olive couch.

He slid off my golf shirt and then I removed his tank top. I noticed the bulge in his pants as I unzipped them and pulled them down to reveal a tented jockstrap.

"Nice, kinky daddy," I said.

"If you think that's kinky," he said in his low voice. "You're in for a long weekend, pup."

He put his thumbs under the elastic and freed his desire as I immediately took that crimson cock into my muzzle. I bobbed back and forth against it, swirling my tongue around it while being rewarded for my eagerness.

"That's the fucking ticket, you little whelp."

We had gone over my limits again those past couple days, and Ezra was kind and understanding about what I was and wasn't willing to do.

The coyote grabbed his green harness along with my leash, collar, and hood from my suitcase in his room. He put the leash on me and walked me around the living room, hallway, and then the kitchen. He found a shiny, silver dog bowl and poured cereal and soy milk into it.

"Come on, Spot. Have some dinner."

He pushed my head into the bowl as it spilled on the floor.

"Such a messy eater! Bad Spot! I'm gonna have to clean this up," he yelled, yanking my collar and then spanking me. "Naughty pups need to be punished."

"Sit and stay!" he commanded, walking away.

I sat and waited as my pink cock bobbed to my heartbeat, dripping pre onto the linoleum.

He came back with a tube of lube and immediately lifted my tail and shoved three fingers into me. The coyote then began lubing himself up.

"This hurts me more than it will hurt you," he said like a disappointed father as I whined. Ezra put the tip of his cock against my entrance, shoving himself deep into me.

I immediately felt so full while taking a sharp breath.

He then pressed his knot into me, and then pulled it out quickly while saying, "Lane told me what you did to him in the bathroom." He kept repeating this and my hole was getting so sore.

"I invite you into this new home and you think you can just make a mess whenever you want?"

I whimpered in response and he kept knotting me and pulling out faster. Soon he kept the plug in me and began grunting. He then tugged the leash as he grunted.

"I'm fucking coming in you, Spot," he growled and then he reached for my groin.

His own knot and cock mashed against my prostate and the stimulation behind my knot made me pant and mewl as the intensity built. The coyote above me was howling and roaring into my ear as the world shook around us. My muscles tensed as pleasure manifested within me and warmth filled my groin. It spread across my belly and throat as I shot a couple loads onto the floor and then panted in pure bliss.

Ezra stepped around, and we were facing away from one another.

"Whoops, I forgot to close the blinds," he said, and I noticed a wolf and lion staring at us from another building. They turned away when we looked at them. Despite the sun being down, the lamp and city lights still illuminated our scene. We laughed it off during our incredibly warm afterglow.

The wallaby and rat's room was rather large and split down the middle with what interested them. The left side was full of black and red. There were old movie posters along with heavy metal concert flyers. The right side of the room was an explosion of neon and highlighter yellow.

"Are you sure you're alright with all of this?" he asked.

"Yeah, I'll be alright," I said with a little nod.

"I don't want a repeat of that bathroom incident."

"It won't happen again."

Bill had taken me to a rage room in downtown Seattle earlier that day to resolve my past conflict. He had told me to imagine all my haters and the people who hurt me in the bottles and furniture I destroyed, and I was feeling good afterwards.

He checked a few things on his computer before the festivities would commence.

"To be honest," he said. "I've been pretty jealous of you."

"Why?"

"Ezra and Lane fell for you so quickly," he said. "It took a year of living here with Lane before we started dating."

"I don't think I tried to do anything..."

"I know," he interrupted. "I guess I've had to deal with my own insecurities. Then there's the whole music thing. I didn't start cello and playing bass guitar until I was in high school, and I never went to music school, so you're miles ahead of me when it comes to musical skill."

"It's not a competition," I said gently. "We're trying to play the best of our abilities together."

"I know you're right, but I really wish things could've been different for me. I sell instruments that I can't even play."

"There's always time to learn and improve."

"That's why people like you, Kyle. You're so sweet and innocent. I think you're hella cute, but honestly, I don't know if I'm really into dating you."

"That's fair," I said, rubbing my arm. "I guess I feel the same."

"This might help calm you down," he said as he played the violin sonata on his computer and turned up the speakers. "Ezra gave me a little tip. Hopefully this helps with the confidence boost."

"Well, I'm working on it," I said. "And getting my anger out was kinda nice."

"No prob," he said and turned off the lights except for the lamp on his nightstand, which he covered with a thin crimson scarf. The lighting was pretty soft, yet erotic as the room was flooded in a pinkish red.

He then took off his flannel, t-shirt and pants; again, no underwear. I then disrobed quickly and donned my blue mask.

The wallaby got onto the bed and slipped on his scarlet and black mask. He spread his legs and let his tail rest between them.

"Suck," he ordered.

"Yessir." I began fellating the chubby wallaby as he moaned.

He yanked my chain and said, "Give me your paw!" He then moved it to his balls and said, "You know what do to."

I nodded.

"Do it like I showed you."

"I guess they wouldn't be called 'balls' if they weren't meant to be played with," I said.

"They wouldn't be called balls if they weren't meant to be struck!"

I held his hefty nuts by the neck of the sack and began gently slapping them.

"Harder!" he yelled as he yanked my leash. "When I want my balls slapped, you need to fucking slap them."

"Yessir," I said as I smacked them with much more vigor with my open palm.

"More!" he yelled after a pained grunt.

I kept hitting them and his cock jumped and spurted pre as Bill made sounds of agony.

After a bit he got up and bent over the bed, resting his forearms on it. The wallaby lifted his tail and showed off his large testicles.

"Remember, no toes, and only the top of your foot."

"Okay."

"Okay, what?" He glared at me.

"Okay, Sir!"

I wound up my leg and landed the blow square to his sac as he fell onto the bed and started coughing.

"Good boy. Do it again!" He readied himself again as I went for another kick.

He held his package and writhed on the bed.

"Are…are you okay?"

"Yes," he whispered. "Don't ruin the mood."

"Oh, okay."

"Grab that book from the desk," he commanded. Atop his mahogany computer desk was a maroon book with a little flame on the cover. It was a hardcover collection of gay, erotic light novels.

I gave it to the wallaby, and he sat up and opened the book so that the back cover was under his bloated balls.

He then said, "Shut the book."

I gulped, but the soothing, playful sonata calmed my nerves, and I quickly closed it on his balls.

He yowled in pain at the impact, threw the book off the bed and started panting. When he came to, Bill glared daggers at me, and I worried I did something wrong.

The wallaby then opened his nightstand and tossed a bottle of red 'Ignite' lube to me. He proceeded to get on all fours atop the bed and lift his tail to reveal a dark, pink pucker as he grinned at me. Bill began stroking his cock and grunting. "Fucking top my ass, pup!" His foreskin glided against his glistening glans.

I whined at the incredible sight before me, and hopped onto him. The bright and jaunty bowing of the viola sonata kept me focused and steady as I thought about myself on the stage performing it. I coated my cock and his hole, and it made my member tingle.

"Get that thick cock in me now!" he yelled, grabbed for my leash and yanked it as I sunk my pink hardness into his needy hole.

"Shove it in, whelp!" he shouted, and I sunk myself all the way to the knot.

I tried to get a steady rhythm and thought about my bowing techniques as I felt his delicious hole squeeze and milk pre from me.

"Faster!" I then bucked harder, increasing my tempo as I made sure to use my full length from tip to knot.

"If you fucking come or knot me too soon, I'm gonna castrate you in your sleep!" Despite inflicting all this pain onto him, he was still in charge of the situation, and I didn't realize being a sub could work this way either.

At that, I kept up the pace and enjoyed the feeling of being inside that chubby rump as the wallaby yanked my collar now and then and slapped me with his giant tail. I kept thinking about myself performing the piece to prevent myself from finishing too soon. Just like in music I had a pace to keep up; no dragging or rushing.

After a while he shouted, "Knot me! I'm close!"

I plunged my plug into him, and it went in surprisingly easily. He started grunting and growling, tightening his grip behind my knot as I began panting and whining. My desire swelled with the passion and volume of the sonata. The wallaby howled as he shook and the pressure in my groin built, feeling the world around me shatter intensely into fractured, shimmering shards. I filled the wallaby's hole and collapsed onto him, and we were lying there in a pleasurable daze, bathed in the soft, warm lighting.

The rest of the weekend he played games on his computer and had an icepack under his heavy balls. He had me sucking him off under his desk as the bluelight of the screen illuminated his face.

"Welcome, everyone, to the Dog Haus quarterly pup show!" the emcee announced. "This time we've classed it up by bringing our string quartet, 'The Seattle Under-Hound!'"

The crowd cheered as we bowed and took our seats on the opposite side of the room from the stage. The bulky pine marten explained the rules of the show, and I was impressed by the first contestant and his handler as they made their way through the obstacle course on the stage. The pup was wearing a purple hood along with a matching harness, jockstrap, and leash. He was a buff tiger, and his handler was an even more muscular, portly badger wearing a violet jockstrap.

We started with *Masquerade* by Khachaturian and Ezra cued us in. He was our handler, but for the performance he wore a green pup hood and a green jockstrap. Lane was in his yellow hood, collar, and a yellow thong. I was in a tight blue speedo, matching my mask and collar. All the wallaby had on was his red pup mask and collar. Bill was definitely getting checked out by some guys in the crowd, but he had his cello between his legs to keep up some form of modesty. Our hoods were also modified so that our own ears peeked out from them in order to hear each other and our own instruments properly.

We ran through a couple different pieces, which were more commonly known, like *Moonlight Sonata* and *Eine Kleine Nachtmusik,* and the contestants on the stage were almost dancing together in an overly dramatic manner.

The ending was when it was time for me to shine. I stood and raised my music stand up as I performed *Viola Sonata in D Minor.* There was a couple consisting of a bull and a lion; the handler and the pup, respectively. The bull was in a tux covering his torso, and his jockstrap had a little bowtie on the pouch. They showed themselves off in an elegant manner, yet showing off their muscles as they ran the obstacle course on the stage.

The crowd cheered for me when I finished the piece, and then it was time for 'Passionate Confession' by Tchaikovsky. Something comforting about wearing the pup mask was that I could be anyone I wanted, and performing in this bar was a marriage of two things I loved dearly. I was in my element as I bowed the strings with ease and got to show off some flourishes, since most people probably didn't know the piece. I let the sad and painful sections be heard, but I made some of the faster phrases brighter. As the last notes rang out, I vibratoed as fast as I could while keeping my right paw as steady as possible while it glided smoothly yet powerfully across the strings.

I opened my eyes as the crowd cheered for me and the contestants took a bow. The spotlight was over me as the contestants left the stage. Everyone was turned around, and I felt my heart swell and my eyes well up. The crowd threw jockstraps and condom packets at my feet.

In the end the staff judges and audiences votes were cast and the muscular fennec fox and chubby otter took first place. They were wearing lights on their harnesses and had a neon themed outfit.

Once the show was done and the staff members left, the four of us stayed behind to practice a bit more and to put our belongings away.

"Are my pups ready to take center stage?" Ezra asked as we all got on our paws and knees. He leashed the four of us as we crawled up the few steps to get onto the stage, and then he proceeded to take off his jockstrap and take the underwear off of Lane and me. "Spot! Apollo! Silly pups, you don't wear underwear."

He proceeded to spank us both.

"We have a job to do tonight, boys. Sparky here needs to be bred," the coyote commanded as the wallaby barked happy and barked at me. "Also, the alpha and omega need to learn a lesson for getting into daddy's underwear drawer."

I whimpered at him, and got hard at the sight of Bill's cheeks wide open for me to plunge right into. His heavy sac was also framed between his chubby thighs. The wallaby growled viciously at me as he lifted his thick tail.

As I inched closer to him he snarled louder and louder at me.

"Either you fuck him or you're gonna get neutered, you little whelp," Ezra shouted.

I crawled as fast as I could and pushed my tip between his cheeks. The wallaby tried to turn around and bite me, but I was about as heavy as he was so my weight kept him down, though he was able to keep his hips up.

"Almost forgot, little pups," Ezra said, running off the stage to grab a bottle from his backpack. He then began lubing up Bill's pucker. He did the same to the rat, who started sniffing my rear. I looked back, seeing the coyote put a silicone knot and ring around the rat's cock and balls. It made it look like he had a knot and it pulled his foreskin back and the ring behind it strapped back around his balls. I then felt Lane's tongue between my cheeks, shivering and moaning in ecstasy.

"Yeah, ohhh," I said and immediately felt a sharp yank on my collar as I yipped.

"Dogs...don't fucking talk!" Ezra roared, and I whimpered, trying to push my cock into the wallaby's ass.

I got my pointed tip in and was able to slide in and out as the wonderful feeling of being surrounded by his warmth made me spurt a few jets of pre into that thick ass. I then felt Lane's fat cock push at my own entrance as the head banged against my rear.

"You did a good job tonight, pup, so you're gonna get a reward from daddy." Ezra slathered the peanut butter flavored lube on his cock and pulled his knot out from his sheath. The coyote had the longest and thickest dick out of the four of us, and he took his time stroking it. "Have your treat, little pup."

His enormous cock glistened under the spotlight, and I realized there was only one light shining on the stage, and I was in the center of it. I then felt the rat's engorged cockhead enter me as I took Ezra's cock into my muzzle.

The coyote stood over the wallaby, shoving his cock in and out of me as I tasted the sweet, saccharine lube mixing with his salted pre as the rat pumped himself furiously into me and biting my shoulder.

Lane's thrusts were forcing me to hump the wallaby, and I realized I was already close, but I wanted to knot Bill first and let everyone topping me finish first. I concentrated on my breathing and being in the moment, just like when I was performing. I told myself to just wait before I blew my load.

I heard the rat gently bark and then whimper as he thrusted faster, shoving his makeshift knot into me. He howled into the air, then his teeth sank into my shoulder as he snarled for a while and went limp. It was sudden, and almost painful, but it felt so good to be full.

Soon the coyote's heavy nuts slapped against my chin faster and faster. He moaned and grunted as his delicious seed flooded my muzzled while I shoved my knot into the beta, who growled at me. I felt my sac tighten and my balls rise as the pleasure and pressure in my groin was too much to handle. I howled in muffled ecstasy as I filled my boyfriends' lover with my essence, my body convulsing while the rat above me held me tightly and the coyote kissed me.

I knew it was out of character, but it was the right thing to do. I began pumping Bill's cock, pulling his foreskin back and teasing the head before going back to stroking him again. I had enough room to do so, since his hips here still up. I was rewarded with him whining in pleasure along with a couple quick squeezes behind my knot.

"Sweet pup," the coyote said with a blissful and gentle expression. "You deserve the spotlight."

Wh♥t You Re♥lly W♥nt

Thïger

I can't remember when the visits at the ranch started. Of course, I can't remember when Laura made me start sleeping on the couch, either, nor when George started coming to the gym. At some point everything stopped making linear sense, and I just accepted the sensations as a whole, getting lost in their whirlwind, embracing the totality of it.

I know that George couldn't get his eyes off of me during training, and that I only know that because I couldn't stop staring back at the jackal. His presence in the building was unmistakable every time, as he carried the smell of countryside with him. I remember the shivering as he patted my back and said I had strong muscles, and having to stop my tail from wagging. I remember going to him to ask for help using the machines more and more often, even though I'd joined the gym earlier; something about his tone of voice was comforting, pushing me to do an extra set, making me feel as if everything was worth it as long as he'd say, "Good job."

I know that Laura was angry at me, but the reasons blend together. I remember the silent treatment, having to sleep on the couch, the shouting bouts. However, I still loved the lizard. I didn't want to give up on her. I wanted to, well...I suppose in the end I just wanted to make her happy, to please her, making everything loop around the same idea. I had to discover myself. I had to become aware of my longing. In the gym, at home, at work, drinking with the guys, I always felt lacking, self-conscious, never content in my own fur. I always felt there was something undesirable about me. I hated staring in the mirror. So I tried to do what was expected of me, like drinking beer when we went out, even though I preferred wine, or taking that well-paid data entry position from Laura's father, even though I had plans to go to college. I had no worth in my eyes, so maybe I could have it in the eyes of others. It lifted the burden of decision-making from me.

Laura didn't like this about me. "Stand your ground for one fucking thing!" she'd yell.

"Okay," I'd whisper back.

"No, don't—don't just say that."

"Sorry."

"And stop saying sorry!"

George seemed to perceive all these things as well, but he wasn't bothered by them. In his eyes, they were endearing, adorable...desirable. He let me know pretty much right away. I'm not stupid; I could see the signs. George went for the kill, though, not being one for subtlety. "You're hot," he blurted out one day, post-workout. I felt my cheeks hot, my tail stiff. "Give me your number."

He didn't say, "Would you like *my* number?" His order was very clear. It didn't leave any space for doubt, allowing me to just obey and clearing the fog of worry that was always present in my mind. "Good boy," he said after I complied. He liked saying that, and I liked hearing it. I couldn't guess what it was a preface to, though.

No, I can't remember when the visits to the ranch started— but I know it was pretty fast. Everything escalated quickly, perhaps even at times where it shouldn't have. George's barn, his home away from home, away from everything, had this feeling of privacy, of intimacy to it. The ride away from the city was so long that it was as if I had left the old me behind, and upon arriving I could be someone new, unfettered by all previous expectations, and admit what I really wanted. Admit that I wanted George, and his messy, spiky, sweaty fur, his sharp, smart eyes, his little peeking fang, that chest he so often exposed by unbuttoning his shirts, that thick musk, and overall—overall I wanted what lay between his thighs, even though I had never thought something like that in my life.

"Really?" said George once. "Never in your life?"

"Well..." I stammered. "Maybe, uh...I guess I remember this one time I stared at the wrestlers on TV as a kid..."

"Go on..."

"And I guess there was Jack..."

George raised an eyebrow. "Jack?"

"My best friend in high school. When we'd do sleepovers, and he'd take his shirt off to change into sleeping clothes, I—his chest, the way it was definedùHe was an athlete, see, kind of the opposite of me, but..." I gulped.

George flashed me a grin, his paws caressing my hair, making me close my eyes with a shiver and stay quiet. "I've noticed what parts of me you prefer, boy," he said. "You do love to touch my pecs. I guess I'm not toned, though. Sorry about that. A flabby adult is all you got."

In response, I simply slid down to my knees, and rested my face in his crotch, which had been naked all along, taking his flaccid cock into my mouth, eyes still closed, just lying there, taking in the taste and smell; dried cum and piss. I let it grow harder at its own pace, letting its length come nearer to my throat, but never moving, never being so disrespectful as to prioritize my comfort over his pleasure. My breath, my life, were second to him.

He didn't move, only reacting with his gasps and husky whimpers, letting his cock be stimulated by my warmth until my saliva fell from the corners of my mouth, and still he didn't move, and I knew this one would be one of the hour-long ones, again.

And if I behaved properly, perhaps he'd let me ride him.

It had started from the very first day we arrived at his ranch. I had a general idea of what would happen, most of my hopes rotating around his cock. What he showed me, however, was different. He wasn't forceful; he told me everything in advance and warned me of the bad sides; he gave me a safe-word and asked me if I was willing to keep an open mind. I saw he was opening his maw to repeat that plea, but I stopped him. I only needed to hear it once. *Yes*, I said, I was willing. The new me that had arrived at the ranch was ready to admit what he wanted; and what I wanted was to stop being me, to be free of my will and make the other—George—happy.

All of the tools were inside his barn. Rope, he used to tie my paws behind my back. A gag—a bit gag—he placed around my mouth, and then he tied reins around it. The crop, he used to, well...

"Walk," he ordered, holding the reins. I tried taking one step, then he hit me with the crop.

"Lift your legs up higher."

Yes, I tried to say as well as I could. Then, the crop again.

"Ponies can't talk."

My vision blurred. Did I want this? What would Laura think if she saw me, being treated like this, simply...simply doing what others ordered? Yet, wasn't that how I had always dealt with her? And it repulsed her, while George wanted it. George wanted me.

I whinnied. The crop didn't come. Instead, I felt George's paw down my back, and his words, "Good boy." I felt a thrill that made me dizzy, and I was instantly hard. I started walking, taking higher steps, keeping my shoulders back, my chest out.

"Good, baby, you're so good." He walked beside me, guiding me with the reins. "Bob your head, now. Give me some more movement." I did so for a while, for a couple of minutes. He seemed delighted. When he stopped for a moment, I neighed and nuzzled him, and I could see he was excited as well. "Now, uh." He had to recollect his voice. "Now, get on all fours."

I was about to mumble a "Yes," but then I remembered my orders. Then, I thought better, and spoke anyway, as well as I could with the gag. When the crop inevitably came, it sent electricity through my body, making me moan. *What would Laura think if she saw me?* Well, what did I always think when I saw myself in the mirror? I hated what I saw, I hated that stupid, flawed carcass, and I had always felt—although I hadn't been able to give words to it until now—that this body needed to be punished.

I got on all fours. George slowly, carefully moved on top of me, then sat on my back. The weight made me gasp.

"Walk," he said, "and stop being a bad pony."

I walked, he rode me, and all the hours of gym, my strong back, were given a purpose. I continued making noises all the while, delighting when I could make him squirm. Feed, silage, wood; their scents were all over me as my face was closer to the ground. As nice as it was, though, I couldn't keep it up for very long. My crawling started wobbling. He noticed, stepping off of me. "You must be tired. You should drink something."

I nodded, panting. He left, I could hear water running, and then he returned with a bucket he placed in front of me. He didn't free my paws nor my mouth. He just stared silently. Despite everything I had done up to that point, I blushed, filled with heat, overwhelmed by the situation. But I really was thirsty. I lowered my head into the bucket, getting my muzzle wet and drinking through the bit gag as well as I could. When I looked up, George had the biggest smile on his face. I forgot about the rough floor of the barn, my tired joints or the water spilling down my chin. I felt at peace, for the first time.

At sunset, still in the barn, George undressed me, always slowly, even tenderly, and then cleaned up my body with a wet cloth. The glowing dusk and the warm breeze that came from outside made the room feel illusory, dreamlike. I felt beloved, and he paid special attention to my penis, which had leaked all day. He stroked me until I came, and I thought how weird that was, that he had had the power all along, ever since first meeting him, yet somehow I had been the first to cum in our relationship. He was sweet like that.

We talked about it all throughout the night, and he encouraged me to voice my thoughts openly—what I had liked, what I had disliked. I asked if I had been the first, and he laughed and said no, obviously, which made me feel pretty stupid. So he decided to make me feel better.

We were lying in bed—me, naked, him, shirtless, but with pants on. My desire to see the lower part of his body was killing me, and he knew it. He decided to grant my wish for being such a good pony. He lay down, put his arms behind his head, and let me knock myself out. It felt too good to be true. My hands immediately grabbed his waistband, but then I thought better, despite my throbbing desire, and I moved up higher to kiss his belly, his chest, his neck fur. The way I was teasing myself made me tremble, but ever since I saw him join the gym I had wanted him this way—every part of him, not just his cock. I kissed and licked and worshipped every inch of his fur, including his pits, full of sweat; always stopping, however, below his face. Somehow, kissing him felt outside of boundaries—I thought that was fine, since I could feel his hard-on poking me...but when I looked up he wasn't smiling. He grabbed my chin, leaned forward and kissed me with a passion that was new, strange, and appealing; the mystery of kissing another man, of feeling his hard edges and hard smell. He pushed his tongue down my throat aggressively, and soon I was whimpering with pleasure.

"You are mine," he said, breaking the kiss with heavy breaths. "And I am yours. Don't hesitate again."

I didn't. I moved downwards, lowered his pants and saw his member, steaming with want. He had no underwear. The first time I saw another man's penis so closely. "Take your time," he whispered. "I'm not going anywhere. Explore as much as you'd like." For countless minutes I stroked every inch of it, of his balls—immense, huge balls; I smelled his cock, pressed it against my face, licked it, tasted it, played with it. Sometimes I'd just lie down next to it, overwhelmed, feeling it throb against my face and taking whiffs. "Knock yourself out," George laughed. "But know this. You're my pony, and I'm going to breed you." He said it as a fact, and I knew it was true.

After sucking on his balls for a long time, something I discovered made me feel soothed and in peace, I was ready. I looked up at him and whinnied. He sat up, placing himself on top of me. He grabbed my hands, placing them above my head. Then he kissed me, and kissed me again, and I felt entirely protected and wanted. Then he lined up his cock on my hole, and he fucked me, no—bred me.

When we were done, he wrapped me in his arms and caressed my entire body. In reality, only he had been done, but feeling his climax had fulfilled me as much as my own orgasm earlier that day. His loving touch throughout the night covered all my other needs.

I started going to George's ranch every weekend. I told Laura it was just guys' nights, but she caused problems from the start. The "guys"' names, whom I made up, were nobody she'd heard of, since all of my friends were her friends first. I made sure to never mention George, and it was all made easier when she accused me of cheating on her with some lizard whore. Lying is always easier when there's a bit of truth in it; there was no other woman.

I continued seeing George at gym during the week and in the ranch during the weekends. The gym was important to strengthen my back muscles. In there, our flirting grew more explicit by the day; George seemed shameless, slapping my ass or wrapping an arm around my neck as we walked in or out together, letting me smell his sweat directly. He didn't care how much I blushed, as long as he could broadcast his ownership. I was, after all, his pony. I started looking into that in my own time; I realized there was an entire community about our kind of relationship, and my dynamic with George was just the tip of the iceberg. My curiosity grew bigger and bigger.

The activities at the barn continued. George quickly picked up on my proclivities—one bad step on purpose here, one half-assed neigh there. The swats of the crop were multiplied, and my moans of pain slowly let themselves be moans of pleasure. Our dynamic extended outside of the barn as well, and I took delight in being naked while he was clothed, cooking for him, grabbing a beer for him, and any other order he might have. What surprised me about him, though, was his affection. He always ended every session with long stretches of cuddling and caressing; he liked to clean my body, he really liked to kiss me, and we never slept without entwining our bodies, usually after sex, so I grew accustomed to smelling his seed and his sweat right on my face until they became a comforting thing, like old friends.

His swings between cold dominance and warm affection dazed me, but they also gave room to new feelings.

I stopped thinking of the physical pain as punishment I deserved, but rather as treats I enjoyed. I stopped thinking of my servitude as a lowly position, but rather as a privilege. I started accepting myself. I looked stuff up on the internet about what we were doing, saw how others handled it, and finally, one night, I made up my mind. I decided to ask George the question.

We were sitting outside, staring at the sky. Away from the city, the stars seemed all the brighter. I could see the beautiful Jackal's face despite no lights being on. I started vocalizing, but I stopped myself, wanting to stare at the details of his expression for a moment longer, while he was distracted with the stars, for one brief, eternal moment.

"George?" I asked quietly.

He turned around, smiling. "What's up, boy?"

"I was wondering...No, what I mean is, I wanted to ask..." I gulped, then got cold feet, coming up with something new. "You said you had other ponies before me. Would you tell me about that?"

He was silent for a moment.

"Not ponies—just the one. He introduced me to the game, and we were a pretty good match. Heh..." I'd never heard melancholy in his voice before. "I screwed things up, though. Took me a while to recover."

"Why, what do you...?"

"What about you, though?" he interrupted. "How are things at home? Laura still being a bitch?"

"No, well, that is...She's fine, yeah."

"Boy, listen to me." I looked up at him, at his bright canine eyes. "Let's make a deal, okay? Not an order—just a promise. I'd like you to be completely honest with me. If you do, then..." He sighed. "I'll be honest with you too, I promise."

"Yes, George," I answered mechanically, used to always saying yes to whatever he asked. But I knew he was serious, so I thought for a moment before speaking. "The truth is...things at home aren't okay. Laura, she used to think I was cheating at her with a lizard, but recently, her story changed. She still believed I was cheating on her, only not with a lizard, but with a mammal."

"Huh."

"Yeah. She's always been insecure about her scales. It was her idea for us to sleep in separate beds, but...seeing her so insecure, so unwanted, so as to think her species was undesirable, almost made me confess the truth."

"Did you?" asked George.

"I told her...I told her I still loved her. And her scales. I said these "weekends with the guys' are just, well, that I need a friend group of my own, disconnected from her. To become my own man."

"That sure as hell ain't a lie."

"Yeah, so... This seemed to please Laura, to disarm her. That night I felt something in the air, something I hadn't felt in a long while. A spark between us. I knew right then that if I made a move, if we stared into each other's eyes a second longer, I could sleep with her again." I breathed out. "And I looked away. I think, after that, it ended between us. We don't talk anymore. She just pretends I'm not there."

"Jesus, man," said George, placing a paw over mine. "You really should have told me. That's no way to live, buddy."

I grinned. That wasn't how I had planned for the conversation to go.

"It's her apartment, though. I have nowhere else to go."

"What about...?" he started, making me gulp.

"That's why I decided not to tell you," I finished, stopping him.

"Ah." His ears dropped.

"But, uh..." I went on, deciding to say what I had in mind from the start. "I wanted to propose something to you. It's something I read online, and I think, well, I think you'd really like it."

"What is it?"

"There's this concept of an, uh, live-in slave. Someone who lives to serve you. It would be like these weekends, only, uh, all week long. I think you...we'd both really like it."

George didn't reply. He seemed stunned at first, and then he covered his eyes.

"Fuck. George, if I said something stupid, just forget it—"

"No, buddy, it's not that. It's just, fuck, I guess I had the wrong idea. About us."

"What do you mean?"

"Maybe the feeling wasn't mutual, but I felt there was more between us than our games. I thought I made it obvious...how much I want you. The way in which I want you."

"Oh..."

"Sooner or later, I always, well... I'm just a really sentimental guy, you know? I develop feelings when I shouldn't. I keep forgetting it's just a kink, just sex, you know." He whimpered a laugh out. I was still processing his words. "The same shit happened with my previous pony. I got too involved, tried to make it more romantic and he, well, he bailed."

"George...It wasn't just sex for me, either."

He looked very seriously at me.

"I always felt it," I spoke slowly. "The love. I just didn't dare think I could be worthy, that it could be mutual, so mentioning my problems at home was too scary. Bringing up living with you."

George's face was glowing.

"You're making me so happy, buddy. You dummy. You should have asked, and I would have let you move in right..."

"Wait," I stopped him. "I love pleasing you. That's why I don't want to just move in. I don't want these deeper feelings to replace what we had, to replace the rides, to become your boyfriend to stop being your pony."

"Nothing would be lost." George spoke thoughtfully. "That's what my previous pony missed. These ways of loving don't have to be mutually exclusive, but, ugh, it's so hard, you know? Threading this line in our world. So hard to strike the perfect balance, and we—we could lose everything. If you trust me enough to take this leap, well...What if I ordered you...? No." He pondered for a moment. "I'm going to say something. I want you to reply what *you* really want, please. Just this once, don't think about pleasing me."

"Okay."

"Okay...I love you."

"I love you, too, George," I said, smiling.

His tail started wagging. He walked up to me, slowly making me rest on the night's cold grass. I shivered, wanting his body to warm me up like a puzzle missing a vital piece. As he undressed himself against the moonlight, he kissed me. It wasn't like a first kiss of newfound love; it was like all the previous ones, because it had always been there. Things stopped making linear sense as I started living in the now. Our bodies became one, and all the while he whispered huskily in my ear everything that I was, and I echoed each sentiment.

My boyfriend.

Your boyfriend.

My slave.

Your slave.

My pony.

Yours.

Good Boy

Faolán

"I can't take this anymore!" Mark shouted as he kicked the door closed and threw his bag onto the dusty floor of his apartment. The brown wolf nearly ripped his coat as he wrestled himself out of it and flung it into the general direction of his coat rack. His amber eyes scanned his mess of an apartment before he walked over to his old couch and crashed down on it, falling face-first into a pillow. It only took about ten seconds for the tears to come this time, which was faster than yesterday, or the day before that.

For weeks on end, his life had been made up of getting up early, making his way through morning traffic, being yelled at by his boss for threatening to miss deadlines, being annoyed at colleagues who didn't have the things he needed, being stressed out by doing project after project, working overtime, and coming home late, only to eat, fall asleep, and doing the same thing all over again the next day. He had no time to clean his house, his social life was pretty much non-existent, and he couldn't even fall asleep without the help of pills anymore. This routine had been wearing him thin bit by bit every day, up to the point where he'd just come home and cry after another day, wondering if he'd have the strength to get up again in the morning. Even the weekends brought him no solace, as his mind was so full with work-related things that he just couldn't relax. A life like this was unbearable for a wolf. Even the most die-hard loner needed to have a certain amount of positive social interaction.

He put a frozen pizza in the oven once he'd forced himself

to get off the couch. After all, nobody would make his food for him. He turned on the TV and sighed as he went through the different channels before turning it off again. He was in no mood to watch more depressive news about yet another supposed terrorist attack, stupid politicians doing stupid things, or threats of war. The wolf couldn't stand the happier shows either. Stupid fake people with forced smiles didn't appeal to him. Not anymore.

To kill time, Mark took his phone out of his pocket to check it for messages. There were some work-related once, but he figured he'd check those out tomorrow. His heart warmed a little at a text he'd received from one of his closest friends, Remy. The marble fox had been shopping and was showing off his new outfits in a series of pictures. The two had been friends for years after meeting at a mutual friend's birthday party. It hadn't taken long for the wolf to consider the fox part of his pack.

"Looking good, cutie," the wolf texted while smiling a little. He made his way back to the kitchen to wait for the pizza there, keeping an eye on the timer.

"Thanks, babe. Now send me a picture of what you are wearing!" the fox texted back after a few minutes.

"Sorry, I'm really not in the mood right now. I look like shit. Maybe later."

"What's wrong, hon? Bad day at work?"

"More like a bad month. I'm seriously thinking about quitting."

The autumn-coloured wolf had expected another text to that, but the fox called him instead. "Oh dear…" he said before taking a deep breath and answering his phone.

"What do you mean quit? You can't quit, you know that!" Remy's high-pitched voice chittered in his ear.

"I know, man, I know. I just don't think I can take this for much longer. I can't eat right, I can't sleep right, I can't even enjoy my weekends!" he whined into the receiving end of his phone. He generally didn't like talking about his problems, as he didn't want to burden anyone else with them, but the wolf knew that Remy would demand him to come clear about it anyway. He loved that about him.

"Hmmm…it's Friday today, so you shouldn't have anything to do tomorrow, right?" the marble fox asked.

Oh, oh…

"Uhm…right?" he said questioningly, wondering what Remy was up to.

"Good! I'll see you tomorrow. I'll be there around twelve, so don't sleep in too much!"

"But…but I eh—" the wolf started.

"Blah blah blah, no buts, mister! See ya, wuffy!" the fox said cheerfully before hanging up the phone.

The wolf moved his phone from his ear and stared at it until his oven signalled that the pizza was ready. Well, at least he wouldn't be alone the next day. That had to count for something.

ΩΩΩ

Being with Remy proved to be enough of a distraction for the wolf to actually have fun for a while. The two friends had crashed onto the fox's couch after a quick trip to the supermarket for some snacks, before putting on a romantic comedy that they'd seen a hundred times already. He chuckled at the same old jokes before his mind wandered back to work again. He sighed deeply and looked down at his paw holding the tiny candy banana he was planning to pop into his mouth. Mark was wondering whether he'd get yelled at again for things other people failed to do. He worked as hard as he could, but if others didn't do their parts, then he couldn't really be blamed for it, right? It wasn't until he looked up again that he noticed the film had been paused.

"Hey, did you pause it?" he asked.

The white fox pouted at the wolf, his lowered eyebrows looked even more menacing due to the black markings in his face. Mark had always thought the markings looked like a double axe. "Yes, I did. Five minutes ago, Mark," Remy said.

"Oh…I… I'm sorry," he said softly, his ears and tail lowering all the way. "It's just that wo—"

He was shushed by the marble fox placing a finger over his lips and giving him a stern look. "I don't want to hear it. Today is about having fun and relaxing. If you can't keep your head away from anything else, I'll be forced to take drastic measures," he said, ending the sentence with a grin on his vulpine face, his yellow eyes twinkling mischievously.

The wolf's ears tilted back and he looked nervous and unsure. "What drastic measures?" he asked.

"Stay there and don't move," the fox said before poking Mark's nose and disappearing upstairs. He returned a minute later with a sports bag, which caused the wolf to frown and tilt his head.

"What's in there? Are we going to exercise?"

"Hmm...not exactly. We're going to clear your head, I hope," he said as he placed the bag on in front of the wolf as he sat down again. "I want you to open this and take out whatever is inside. If you have any questions, I'd like you to ask them," Remy said with a serious look in his eyes.

Mark could tell the fox was excited by the wagging of his tail, so he wondered what was inside the bag. His interest was piqued, to say the least, so he slowly unzipped the black bag, hoping that nothing would jump out at him. When this didn't seem to be the case, he reached in with his dark brown paw and took out a dog collar with a snowflake-shaped tag on it that read "Snow".

"This is a collar. I didn't know you had a dog," he said as he put it aside and reached in again, retrieving a light blue dog harness next. He checked it out with both paws and frowned a little. "A big dog, apparently," he muttered before reaching back in, wondering if he'd find a food bowl next. Remy still hadn't uttered a word, even though he seemed a little nervous, though thrilled.

The brown wolf's paw didn't find a bowl though, and he picked up a small item his fingers had wrapped themselves around. He took it in both paws and moved it closer to his face so he could take a better look at it. It was made of leather and about the size of his fist. "Is this a...glove?" he asked while looking at his friend.

The fox nodded. "It's called a mitten," the marble fox said as he moved a little and sat down on his paws.

"There's no room for a thumb though," Mark noticed as he looked at the curious item. He reached into the bag and took out a second one. He couldn't see a dog wearing this at all. After all, why would it? What purpose did it serve? "Remy, you don't have a dog, do you?"

The fox giggled and shook his head. "Haven't had one ever since I moved out to live by myself."

Staring at the items around him with an intense frown, which was known to Remy as his 'thinking face', the wolf could only come to one other logical conclusion. "Remy, this is going to sound strange, but...do you wear these yourself? Are they yours?"

The lithe fox grinned and nodded. "I do. I participate in puppy play," he explained. "As soon as I put on this gear, I am no longer Remy. Instead, I'll be a puppy by the name of Snow."

"And...then what? You behave like a feral dog? Will you play fetch and sleep in a doggy basket?" the wolf asked with a frown on his face. It just seemed really weird to him. It wasn't that he had a problem with his friend being into this. It was just that he'd never encountered anyone who did this before.

Remy nodded and giggled. "And bark, beg for belly rubs, and play with other pups."

"Why did you pick a nickname? Wouldn't it be easier to just use your normal name? After all, you're pretty much used to it, right?"

"Having a nickname helps me get into character. Sure, there are many pups who just use their own names, but I feel that I can get into my head space easier by using a different name," the white fox said.

"Head space?" Mark enquired.

"The thing that you have been so thoroughly lacking lately, my friend. It's like a sort of trance, almost. It's really difficult to explain, but if I get into my head space, I let go of all of my worries and forget about them for a while. It's strangely relaxing. Pups don't have to worry about bosses, colleagues, workload, bills, and other things like that. We are free from all that."

"Sounds like a dream to me," the brown canine said before

taking the collar in his paws again and looking at it. What would it feel like to wear this? Would it feel weird or comfortable? "Since you're a puppy, do you also have someone who takes care of you? A master of some kind?" he asked.

"Not at the moment, no. A lot of pups do, but some of us, me included, like the idea of being free more. I'm pretty sure I'll end up with a nice handler again sometime, but there's no need to rush."

"And what do they do? Tie you up and have their way with you?" Mark asked as he put the collar down again and picked up the weird-looking mittens once more, looking them over and trying them on. Well, one of them, since he couldn't close the second by himself. He felt that his thumb was rendered useless, which was quite annoying.

"You're thinking about BDSM or S&M even. It's not like that. Sure, there's a large part of the puppy community that are totally into engaging into sexual activities with their handlers or each other, but others just do it because they want to escape their normal lives for a while. The relationship between a puppy and his or her handler is about trust and love. Sex can be a part of that relationship, but it's not a requirement," Remy calmly explained while smiling.

Mark felt that he couldn't stop listening to what his friend had to say. It all sounded so good to his ears, and he was definitely intrigued. It helped that Remy was so passionate about it all. It made the brown wolf want to try it for himself. If it would help him get away from the frustration of his boss's lack of proper leadership, then he'd be all for it.

"Do you have sex while being a puppy?" he asked as he narrowed his eyes playfully.

"Heh, what do you think?" the marble fox answered with a smirk on his face as he wiggled his eyebrows.

The wolf chuckled and rolled his eyes. "Foxes... I should've known."

"Asshole," the smaller male said before giggling. "Anyway, want to try it on? I can see in your eyes that you are interested, dear. Just give in," he said as he held up the harness.

After clearing his throat and looking away while blushing, Mark eventually nodded. The harness came on first, and despite it mostly consisting of straps and metal rings, it was definitely comfortable. The light blue didn't go with his fur that well, but he'd just have to ignore that. The gear wasn't his anyway. The mittens came next, and they rendered him helpless. He nearly automatically moved onto all-fours while looking at his friend, who was very gently stroking his neck and shoulders. It felt nice to be touched like that, especially after the hard time he'd been through recently. Remy took a pair of knee protectors out of the bag as well and put them on the taller male. They would protect his knees when he'd walk around on all-fours. The collar came last, a leash attached to it, and even that piece of gear fit very comfortably around his neck, even though it wasn't designed for his size. It somehow made him feel...special? He certainly felt more submissive than without the collar. It was amazing what a simple piece of leather could do to someone.

"I normally never let other people wear my collar, but I'll make a special exception for you today, Mark," he said and smiled. "How are you feeling?"

The wolf actually had to think about that for a bit, and he rolled his shoulder until they popped. "Well...I feel...lighter? Does that make sense? It feels like I'm going to play an exciting game, or as if I'm about to visit a theme park. I know that sounds strange, but it's the same sensation for me. It's comfortable. The petting feels really nice too," he said and moved a little closer to his friend, who continued petting him.

"You act like a natural puppy, cutie. I think this could very well be a really good thing for you. Something that will help you cope with the unfairness in your life. Come. I have something else to show you," the vulpine said as he stood up and walked over to his computer.

"Uhm...do I walk on two paws or on four?" Mark asked.

"Good question, puppy. That's up to you to decide. I'm fine with you doing either."

Mark nodded and got up from the couch, walking over to the fox the way he'd normally walk. He wasn't sure enough about this situation that he'd walk around on his hands and knees. He joined Remy at his computer and took a seat next to him, which was harder than he thought without the use of his thumbs. He guessed the saying was true: a man only truly appreciates something after he has lost it.

Remy opened a website that automatically logged him in. On it were a lot of pictures of people wearing the gear he was currently wearing, and more. Some were even wearing some sort of masks that gave them a canine appearance. He could tell from their tails that they weren't though. "What is this, Remy?" he asked as he kept his eyes on the screen as his friend scrolled through the timeline.

"This is a social media website called 'Pupper'," he said with a smile. "What do you say about making an account for you? You seem to be taking to this rather naturally, considering that you've never even heard of all of this before," the smaller male said. "It must be because you're naturally inclined to act submissive, being an Omega."

His words brought a slight blush to the wolf's face, and he scratched himself behind his ear, which felt really strange now that his paws were covered by the leather mittens. He frowned and pouted at the gear before looking at his friend again. "I don't know, man. I… It's all going a bit fast, isn't it? I mean…this is nice and all, but it's really awkward too. I'm only doing this now because I trust you," he said, looking troubled as his ears lowered a little.

The marble fox turned to him and placed his paws on the canine's cheeks, stroking them while his yellow eyes gazed into Mark's amber ones. "Alright," he said softly. "You are coming with me next week though. The monthly puppy night will be held that night, and I want you to come with me to check it out. You won't have to participate in anything if you don't want to, but please come with me. It's the best way to find out if you'll like all of this or not."

The brown male's eyes grew a little bigger as he took in the fox's request. "Where will this take place?" he asked.

"In the house of one of the local masters. He has enough

space to host us. There will also be enough extra gear for you to try things out if you're up for it."

The idea of going to a party liked that made the wolf uncomfortable to say the least. It was all just so strange to him. He'd never known that a community like this even existed, and now he found out that his friend was part of it and the fox was planning on taking him to see a whole group of them at a party a week later? The entire situation felt unreal to him, like a dream. There was only one way to find out if this dream would turn out to be a nightmare or not.

"Alright, but I want you to stick to my side that night, and…and I want a name too. A puppy name. I feel uncomfortable using my real name. What if someone there is connected to my job somehow? I don't need an extra stress factor right now," he spoke as he stated his terms.

"Heh, sure thing, until you find someone else you want to stick to," the fox said with a teasing grin on his face, which got the wolf to pout at him. "What name would you like then?"

"Well, my mother once told me that if my dad hadn't pushed for the name Mark, that my name would probably have been Bobby. Do you think that's a good name?" the wolf asked as he thought about it. He didn't want to use the names of other feral pets he used to have. That would just have been too awkward for him personally.

"Oh! That's a really good one, actually! It sounds so cute! To be honest, I think that name might actually suit you better than Mark!" he said and giggled with enthusiasm. "Alright, I'll just call you Bobby at the party then."

"Thanks. Can you take these off now? I think I'll head back home now," Mark said while wagging. He felt very excited about going to a party with the fox. He imagined adults on all-fours barking and getting attention from the masters. He wondered if it reflected what he would see next weekend. He'd just have to wait and see.

The week leading up to the puppy night was a blur to Mark. It was the same old yelling and screaming, but he wasn't that affected by it, it seemed. He was much too distracted by the thought of going to the party, so he didn't even think of feeling down. He smiled to himself as he had that thought, and filed it away as a good thing. He took a left turn and drove down the road. His eyes scanned the area before he looked at his GPS. He'd reach the place in approximately two minutes. His heart started beating faster in anticipation of what was to come. Would it really be as he'd imagined so many times? Would people be naked? What species should he expect to see there? Would it be scary or awkward? Would he fit in?

"You look really cute when you're worrying like that," Remy said while grinning as he stretched his lithe body in the passenger seat. The little twink was only wearing a pair of hotpants, and his harness. It looked absolutely fantastic on him, but the wolf couldn't help but wonder if this was really okay. Surely, this didn't count as an outfit, did it?

"Shut up, Remy, I'm trying to concentrate," the brown canine said while blushing slightly. Even after all this time, the fox's compliments always managed to catch him off-guard.

The marble fox reached into his bag and took out his light blue collar. He put it on and wagged happily before looking at you. "Call me Snow, Bobby," he said teasingly before fluttering his lashes at his friend, who missed it because he was being a responsible driver. "We will refer to each other by our pup names for the rest of the night, alright?"

"Fine. Shut up, Snow," he said before chuckling a little. It still felt silly to refer to his friend that way. Perhaps if he saw it as a nickname, it wouldn't feel as strange. Nodding to himself while taking a right turn, he decided that he'd view it as such. "Now, where is this handler's house we are supposed to go to?" he asked.

"It's at the end of the street. You really can't miss it," Snow said while carefully giving his chest and stomach, as well as his legs, a final brushing. It wasn't until the end of the street that Bobby knew how right he was.

The word 'house' really didn't do the place justice, as the place was more like a mansion than anything else. It was completely surrounded by a pointy fence, so it was free from having any direct neighbours. Bobby surely felt out of place at the sight of it. He parked the car at the gate and got out after Snow had already done so. The friends walked up to the imposing iron gate. A camera was trained on them and Snow waved happily at it. "Good evening, sir! We are Snow and Bobby, and we've come for the puppy night!" he stated. Bobby winced at the fox's loud voice and looked around to see if anyone could have heard them.

The gates opened automatically, granting the friends access into the lofty home. After walking down the road leading to the front door, they were greeted by their generous host, a dapper-looking cat, his fur black and white, and his eyes a piercing blue. "Good evening, Snow, how are you? I take it that this is your friend Bobby?" he asked, speaking with a rather posh British accent.

Bobby blushed slightly and nodded, his ears and tail lowering slightly because of the nerves he was experiencing. Even though the man obviously wasn't a wolf, there was something about him that radiated authority, which the brown wolf was very sensitive to. He kept his eyes on the ground out of respect.

The cat just smiled at that and nodded his head only once. "It's nice to meet you, Bobby. My name is Mr Blackstone, and you two will be in my care tonight," he said before stepping to the side, revealing his lobby. "Please, come in and join the others. The restroom is behind the first door on your right; the dressing room is behind the second door. The rest is in the basement behind the first door on your left. You are not to wander around the house without explicit permission from me. Do you have any questions?" he explained calmly with the hint of a smile on his face.

Snow and Bobby shook their heads and headed for the dressing room after the cat had turned away from them to head to the basement. The room was frugally decorated, with only some chair and benches along the walls. "This is all so strange still. Is Blackstone English or something? He both dresses and stands like a butler, but he's the owner of this place, right?"

Bobby asked.

Snow nodded while checking himself out in a large mirror. "Yeah, he's something else alright. He's a very kind man though. Super intelligent too! I believe he's a professor at the university," he said. "Say, if you want to put on some gear as well, there's a box with stuff over here," he said as he tapped a wooden box with his foot. He took his mittens out of his bag and handed them to Bobby. "Can you put these on me, please?" he asked.

Bobby nodded and did as Snow asked before looking at the gear in the box. "I...I don't know yet. Maybe later. Shall we go to the basement?"

"Oh? Someone sounds eager."

"Shut up! I just... Urgh, forget it. Let's go," he said as he opened the door and walked out. Snow followed him on all fours, his tail wagging happily as he barked at Bobby. It seemed the fox was in his head space already. The two headed down to the basement. What greeted them there was unlike anything Bobby had imagined for the past week. The room was simply huge, and filled with various things that reminded him of his childhood. There was a ball pit, a bouncy castle, pillows spread all over the floor, which was covered in soft mats. Everything was incredibly colourful, and pups of all species were moving around, playing in the aforementioned areas, or curled up on the pillows, often not alone. He spotted several felines, and even a lizard! He even spotted two female puppies, which surprised him. He'd thought that puppy play was mostly a gay thing. Apparently, he was wrong about that. Watching all those puppies interact with each other and the handlers was a little like watching a nature documentary. A very strange one at that. Were it not for the handlers standing and sitting around the room, enjoying drinks, he'd have felt terribly overdressed. The wolf had thought that Snow was underdressed, but a lot of the pups wore even less, as around half of them were downright naked.

Despite the strangeness of it all, the overall feeling in the room was one of happiness and relaxation. There was no sign of negative tension in the air, and everyone seemed very comfortable with each other. He looked next to him to see that the fox had already left to join the others in their games. The white fur was easy to spot, and the autumn-furred wolf found his friend on the bouncy castle, nuzzling a snow leopard before pouncing on him. Bobby chuckled at that and watched the two with a bright smile on his face.

"Cute, aren't they? I didn't know Snow had a handler now," a deep voice spoke to his left. He turned his head to look at a large black wolf who had his aquamarine blue eyes focused on him. "Oh eh, I'm not his handler. I'm…not a handler, actually," he said and rubbed the back of his head as confessing that got him a little nervous again.

"Not a handler? Are you a puppy then? You certainly are cute enough," the man said with a warm smile on his strong face. His broad muscled frame was hugged by a tight black tank top that read "ALPHA" on the chest.

"I'm not sure yet," Bobby said truthfully while looking away shyly, blushing brightly at the man's compliment. It was quite obvious the man saw himself as the leader of a pack with a shirt like that. He had a dominant aura about him as well, but it was different from Blackstone's, as if this man ruled with a soft, yet firm touch. He kind of felt more like a father figure than a leader, Bobby thought.

"Ah, you're new at this then. Come, sit with me, eh…"

"Bobby," the wolf said, feeling strangely comfortable using that name there. He sat down on the couch, but made sure there was some physical space between the two of them still. After all, he didn't know the guy, even though he was a total dreamboat and seemed nice.

"Such a cute name. My name is Richard. Would you mind telling me how you came in contact with the pup scene, Bobby?" the black canine asked.

The younger male turned a little to put the large wolf in his full view, making sure not to meet his eyes directly though, even though he really wanted to look into those gems some more. "Snow introduced me to it after I complained about not knowing whether I could go on with my life the way it was. My job was driving me crazy and left me with little else to do or even think about. Snow figured this was a good way to forget about my worries for a while," he explained. It was only afterwards that he wondered why he was so open about his problems to this man. He was usually quite a reserved person, who only confided in his friends. He couldn't put his finger on it, but there was something about this man that made him want to trust him. How strange. Could it be the Alpha thing?

Richard nodded while listening, his blue eyes never leaving Bobby's. "It's quite a common reason why people try out puppy play. It's a form of escapism after all. Just, instead of grabbing a bottle or losing all your money by gambling, you take on the role of a puppy. It's a much healthier alternative, if you ask me," he said and smiled. "Do you have a Pupper account?"

The smaller wolf found himself agreeing with the man, and he was nodding away while wagging, until the handler's question finally reached his brains. "Oh, no, not yet. I want to see how tonight goes first," he said.

The man leaned back and turned his eyes back to the crowd. "Well, it seems tonight is definitely going to be a lot of fun," he said with a smirk on his face."

Bobby turned his attention back to the group of puppies, only to have his jaw dropping by what he saw. In the short time he'd been talking with Richard, Snow had somehow managed to shed his last bit of clothing, and was being mounted by a lion wearing a puppy hood. The lion had a leash attached to his collar, which was held by a tough-looking lioness. "Good boy!" she cooed while grinning.

After the initial shock of his best friend having sex in the middle of a room of people, Bobby noticed the lion had a padlock on his collar. When he looked around, he noticed that at least five other pups had the same accessory. "Uhm, Richard, why do so many pups wear a padlock?" he asked softly.

"It means they are owned by a handler, and that you can't play with them unless you have the handler's permission," he said before unzipping his faded grey jeans and reaching into his red black boxerbriefs to stroke and knead his fat sheath.

Bobby found himself transfixed on the man's crotch. He

found himself lusting after the man, and he was almost on all fours when the man pushed a finger against his nose.

"If you want to play, you first need to get into your proper uniform, puppy," the black wolf said with a grin.

Understanding those words, Bobby nodded and quickly left the basement for the dressing room. He stripped down to his underwear immediately and giggled nervously at his own enthusiasm. This was all so unlike him. Well, unlike Mark. Perhaps it was exactly like Bobby. He found a spare green leather collar in the gear box and put it on before putting on a matching green harness. He found black leather mittens as well, but he couldn't put those on himself. He whimpered softly before turning around at the sound of the door opening. In walked Mr Blackstone, who smiled kindly at the brown puppy.

"I see you have decided to join in, Bobby. Allow me to help you with your mittens," he said as he walked over. After rendering his hands useless, the black-and-white cat strapped some protectors to his knees as well. "Wouldn't want you to hurt your knees, would we?" he asked before spanking the pup's rear, drawing a surprised yelp from the pup. "Now, have fun, pup," he said as he held the door open.

The green puppy went back down to the basement and went down on all fours as he made his way back over to Richard. He could see that the lion was still on the marble fox, the sound of their bodies slapping together creating a special kind of music the wolf was quite unfamiliar with. He hadn't had sex in a very long time, and now it was right in front of him, in the shape of a large muscular handsome black Alpha wolf, who was currently stroking a rather engorged red length.

The man looked down at him and smiled that easy smile again, before reaching out and petting him. "Such a pretty puppy. Do you want this?" he asked as he teasingly waved his cock in front of Bobby's nose. Bobby nodded and whined softly. It felt a little embarrassing to do this, but knowing what was in it for him quickly made him push those feelings far down. "You'll have to earn it first though. Sit," Richard commanded.

Bobby tried his best to copy the way feral dogs sat on the

floor, and wagged happily. There were no obstructing thoughts floating around in his mind any longer. The only thing that mattered was pleasing this man, so he would get rewarded.

"Paw."

Heh, easy. Bobby placed his right paw in the man's hand.

"Other paw."

Putting down his right paw again, the brown wolf moved his weight on his right side and placed his left paw in the man's hand.

"Down," Richard said while pointing down at the floor.

The pup completely flattened himself against the floor in a way similar to how dogs lay down when they wanted a treat.

"Very good. Roll over, pup," the man ordered, causing the happy puppy to roll over onto his back, paws in the air, bulge exposed, and his tail thumping against the floor. "It seems you're a true natural, puppy. Up. You've earned your reward," he said as he spread his legs and drank some of his beer.

Bobby crawled back up as fast as he could and buried his nose in the handler's sack, sniffing so deeply that he could taste the man's musk on his tongue already. This only fuelled his hunger even more. After another few good deep sniffs, the puppy started licking Richard's length, using his long smooth tongue to the best of his ability. He pressed the thick cock into the man's abs with his cold nose, drawing a soft gasp from the black wolf, only to have him moan as Bobby's tongue snaked out to cover the quivering member again.

"Hmmff…you're talented, puppy. You are definitely a good boy," Richard said while placing his paw on Bobby's cheek, stroking his face gently before scratching at just the right spot behind his ear. The pup curled his tongue underneath the red cock, only to scoop it up so he could finally wrap his soft lips around it. He was so eager that he nearly choked himself on it as he deep-throated the guy, causing tears to well up in his eyes. He coughed a little before suckling gently on the tip, his amber eyes on the handler's blue gems. "Careful there, puppy. I don't want you to get hurt," he said softly while petting the younger male between his ears, gently raking his black claws through the fur, leaving subtle trails that were smoothed over by his palm.

Bobby was blushing brightly from the way Richard treated him. Not only were they engaged in a very intimate and lewd activity, but, more than that, the larger wolf was making sure he was comfortable and relaxed. If he'd wanted to make the pup feel loved, he had doubtlessly managed to do so, and the puppy rewarded him by bobbing his head along his shaft, slobbering and sucking as his tongue worked the underside of that tasty meat.

"Hmmff, alright, Bobby, that's enough for now. Let's go somewhere more comfortable," he said before taking a chain out of his pocket. He leashed the smaller male and led him to the bouncy castle. On their way there, Bobby turned his head to look at Snow and the lion, who had ceased their activities and lay cuddled up on one of the large pillows. The lioness was petting them and brushing their fur. The marble fox looked close to sleeping, but he managed to flash a bright smile at his friend, knowing what was about to transpire, judging from the quivering red rocket between the brown wolf's legs.

Richard led the puppy onto the bouncy castle while idly stroking his slick cock, still wet with the smaller canine's saliva. The two female puppies, a tigress and an otter, were cuddled up in the corner and seemingly lost in each other. They looked up when they felt the displacement of air in the castle and briefly looked at the two males before resting their heads back on the colourful PVC surface.

Having the females' eyes on him, even for a short moment, made Bobby feel a little self-conscious, even though he was still extremely excited about what would undoubtedly come next. He playfully bounced on the stretchy surface below, wagging happily. The rookie pup turned around to the wolf holding his leash and gave the man's cock a few more licks before looking up expectantly.

The black wolf looked down and smiled before pointing his fat cock down, poking the pup's nose with it. "Lube it up well, puppy. You'll need it," he said before menacingly licking his teeth, which only served to turn the pup on more. He took the rod in his muzzle and suckled gently, making sure to apply enough tongue, slobbering his saliva all over the large wolf's length. It had been a long time since he'd last been topped, but he was sure Richard would treat him well.

He tried to take the knot into his muzzle as well, but the handler pushed him down before he would accidentally scrape him with his sharp fangs. "Turn around, handsome," he said as he slowly went down on his knees. "Only the best puppies get this kind of reward, Bobby, but I think you've earned it, right?" he asked.

He blushed brightly at those words but wagged strongly before barking and pushing back against the man, who spanked him gently and pushed him back. "Patience, Bobby," he said with a slight chuckle. The black canine gently kneaded the wolf's round rump before spreading the cheeks and pushing his warm cock up between those two wonderful mounds. He took a small bottle of lube out of his pocket and poured the cold substance onto his cock, letting it dribble down and smearing it across the pup's ass, causing him to gasp and yip. After putting the lube away, the man took hold of the smaller male's hips and started grinding up under his tail, squeezing his thick member between the fluffy brown buns.

The hotdogging further strengthened the pup's need, which he showed by actively pushing back against the man. He wanted to be dominated by this male, and he would do whatever he'd demand of him to make it happen. He ground his hips back in circles, making sure to mash the black wolf's length between the soft flesh of his rump and Richard's firm abs. He regretted not being able to touch himself at that point, but this only made it all the more clear that he was at the handler's mercy, an idea that pushed all the right buttons.

After a few minutes of this, the red flesh was aimed at the brown male's slick pucker. The man forced the pup's head up by pulling on the leash. It had been a while since a pup, and especially a new one, had Richard this fired up. He would enjoy this, and hopefully manage to convince Bobby to meet him again at a later date. He showed great promise, and was way too cute for his own good. He lovingly stroked the pup's bubble butt, and smiled to himself. "Clench down as tightly as you can and as long as you can for me, Bobby."

Despite not having had sex for quite some time, the younger wolf knew about this little trick. He clenched down as much as he could, until his muscles let go on their own, causing them to relax. Richard picked this moment to push into him, sinking his cock in about halfway, stretching out the pup without causing him any pain. Bobby moaned loudly and whimpered as he tried to handle the pleasure coursing through his body. He'd have bit the pillow if he'd had one at that moment.

"Oooh! Such a good puppy!" the black wolf groaned. He growled lustfully and took the leash in his muzzle so he had both paws free. He placed them on Bobby's hips and pulled the wolf back against him, thrusting almost all the way in at the same time, drawing another bark from the male. Richard ground his fat knot against the pup's rump as he let him get used to his cock. "Are you doing okay, Bobby?" he asked after he let go of the leash.

The evident concern for his well-being sent a swarm of butterflies to stir in his belly. The smaller canine nodded and barked while wagging happily. He was doing just fine.

"Glad to hear it," Richard said while smiling, before taking hold of Bobby's tail and setting a gentle pace, using the entire length of his cock. He pulled all the way out of the warm body, before pushing all the way back in. He looked down and grinned at the sight of the pup's ass accepting his cock this readily. There was no doubt that Bobby was enjoying this just as much as he was, judging from the cute sounds that escaped the pup's muzzle.

Quickening his pace caused the sounds to grow both in volume and frequency. Over the course of what seemed to be only five minutes, but what had in fact been much longer, the handler had picked up the pace every few minutes, only to end up really slamming his meat into the eager recipient. The swollen knot ground up against the pup's sore rump with each thrust, causing the smaller male's cock to jump and spurt more pre onto the smooth PVC under him, adding to the small pool that had collected over the course of their lovemaking. Bobby was close to his release, but he wanted to hold out for Richard, hoping they could finish together.

Trying to hold out caused his sphincter to clench down on the handler's cock, which made the man groan and thrust even harder. His breathing was quickening, as was his heart rate. It wasn't long before the man let out a dominating howl and slammed his fat knot inside of the boy's rump, seeding the pup and pulling him against his hard body by his hip and tail. He could feel his cock pulsing against the warm slick muscles that hugged his length, milking him of his seed as the boy came hard, shooting his seed up between his arms and onto the surface of the bouncy castle.

Bobby howled softly in comparison to Richard, not wanting to challenge the man in any way. Even in his current role, ancient wolf instincts were deeply instilled in his being. It made it easier for him to accept the man mating him and filling him up with his sperm. Bobby was an Omega, and he was well-aware of this, so having an Alpha inside of him could only be considered an honour. He worked to please the man even post-orgasm, wishing to have as much of the black wolf's essence inside of him as he could. He swayed his hips and tugged on the knot while clenching down on it as well. He couldn't remember ever been this hungry for anyone before.

Richard pulled the pup up onto his knees and nibbled on his neck, placing soft kisses on it as well. "You're such a good boy, Bobby. I hope we'll be able to do this again soon," he murmured in the wolf's ear. Bobby smiled happily and nodded, his tail thumping against the handler's side. Sometime during their lovemaking, the two females had gotten up and left. Seeing as they would be stuck together for a while, the two curled up together in the corner of the bouncy castle, enjoying their blissful private moment of warm relaxation.

On the way back home, Mark happily hummed along with the radio, something he hadn't done in a long time. "So, Remy, are all pup parties like this one?" he asked with somewhat of a smirk on his face while trying to concentrate on the dark road in front of him.

"Hmm? Nah, most are very tame and only focus on the

social aspect of being a puppy or a handler. I figured I'd take you along to one of the more fun ones though," the marble fox replied with a grin.

"Why did you throw me in the deep end right away, instead of easing me into the scene by taking me to a tame party?"

"Because I was convinced you needed to get laid, and, as it turns out, I was right."

Mark shifted his weight a little and bit his lip. His rump was sore from Richard's impressive knot. It was a pleasing burning sensation though, especially because it reminded him of what had caused it. His phone vibrated in his pocket and the brown wolf moved his paw over it, knowing the message had to be from the black wolf, whom he had exchanged contact details with after the party.

"So, will you come with me again next time, so you can play with that hunk again?" Remy asked before giggling.

Mark stopped at a traffic light and looked over his shoulder to see the same green gear he'd been wearing in a bag on the backseat. "I have a feeling I will," he said, already looking forward to the next time he could be Bobby.

The Wingman's Pup

Jaden Draekus

"Viper One, docked." *Home at last.* Drake sank into his seat as the tension of the ten-hour patrol drained out of him as his starfighter settled to the flight deck of the *Intrepid*. Then the wolfox sighed. *Shit.*

He reached up and pushed the release on his helmet, made sure his ears were properly positioned, and slid it off as the cockpit popped open.

"Commander," the weasel tech reaching in to help with his restraints greeted. "Any problems?"

"Clear across the board. Resupply should be uneventful," the wolfox replied. He took the offered paw and stood upright. "Good to be back on deck."

"Yes, sir."

Drake climbed down the ladder as the weasel plopped into the pilot seat to conduct the post-flight maintenance analysis. The wolfox took a quick glance at the cockpit but continued on—the chief in charge of the maintenance crews said hovering made the techs nervous. *Just when killing time would be useful.*

Around him, similar scenes were playing out on the other three fighters of his flight. The wolfox paused to stretch, getting all the way on his claw tips to work the tightness out of his back. Behind him, his tail wagged as he contemplated a shower and down time then slowed as he remembered what that would entail. He made his way across the hangar, towards where the other three members of One Flight were conversing.

"Commander," Silver, the vixen whose call sign came from

her fur color, greeted. "You look like hell."

Next to her, the other fox, Crimson, nodded in agreement. The raccoon, Wash—Drake's wingman—grinned in a way that reminded Drake exactly what his boyfriend had planned. As a group they started moving to the door.

"Long flight," Drake replied, wincing internally. "Everything good?"

"All good," Crimson said, looking at his wife and Wash for confirming nods. "Everything's filed; all that's left is to brief the next patrol."

Bingo. Drake let his shoulders slump a little in what he hoped looked like exhaustion. "Right. I should go take care of that."

"Colt's leading that one," Wash put in. "So, shouldn't be much of a briefing. One of us can handle it."

"Yeah," Drake said hesitantly. "But he's still new. I'll do the brief."

Silver and Crimson cocked eyebrows and shook their heads in unison. Wash outright frowned. *They're not buying it. Stay on track.*

"Com'on boss," Silver said. "It's nothing special. Let me and Crim take care of it. You and Wash can run along, have fun."

Drake glanced over at the raccoon, wondering just how much his boyfriend had shared with the vixen. "No. I'll do it. Shows I take it seriously."

"That's bullshit and you know it," the raccoon growled.

"He's right, Commander," Crimson said, his tone diplomatic. "Us doing the briefing shows you trust your subordinates."

"I trust you." Drake laughed. *Cut it out. Why can't I just avoid a situation by doing my job?* "Otherwise I'd be flying every mission. Let's get the brief over with."

They gave him unconvinced looks, but the conversation broke up. Crimson and Silver headed off towards the direction of the mess hall, leaving the wolfox and the raccoon alone in the isolation corridor between the hangar and the rest of the ship. Drake turned to depart as well when a paw locked on his arm. The wolfox turned and found himself face to face with a raccoon bristling with anger and frustration. His teeth were bared, and for a heartbeat, Drake actually felt nervous. *Fuck!*

"Remember what you agreed to do?" Wash whispered. "This isn't a good start."

"I didn't forget," the wolfox muttered. "I just don't know if I want to go through with it…"

"Typical," Wash sighed. "I don't know why I expected anything else." He turned and headed towards the door.

"Where are you going?"

"I don't know. Maybe I'll go draft my request for reassignment. Get away from a relationship where my boyfriend can't have any fun at all."

Drake winced as the door closed behind the raccoon. Part of him wanted to be angry, but he couldn't shake the feeling that Wash was right. He took a deep breath, straightened up, and headed to the ready room. At least as a starfighter commander, he didn't have those self-doubts.

The nerves returned an hour later when Drake headed to the locker room and shower that he shared with the rest of the members of One Flight. No one was around as he pulled his supplies out of his locker. The wolfox let out a nervous sigh. *Is it bad I hope he's too mad at me to go through with it? All that delay, and I still don't know if I can.* Drake stripped, visited the attached restroom, made some preparations, and then headed into the shower. His heart was already racing, and his tail twitched behind him.

Drake put his soap on the ledge and was programming in the shower settings when he heard someone enter behind him. He sniffed but couldn't tell who it was, the scents of tile and metal cleaner—as well as scent neutralizing soaps—made it almost impossible to identify anyone by smell in the showers. The commander didn't respond to the presence, respecting what little privacy could be had in a semi-public shower, but it turned out that the other person had no such reservations. Drake felt a larger body press up against his. Since only four people used this locker room and shower, Drake guessed who it was before they spoke.

"Mmmm. Hello there Foxy," Wash whispered, his muzzle slowly pressing into Drake's neck. Any traces of his earlier anger seemed to be gone.

A bit of the tension drained from Drake, at least about Wash being angry. His chest was hammering as he remembered what his boyfriend wanted to do next. *I don't know, Ringtail.* The raccoon's arm wrapped around the wolfox's chest as his tongue pushed into the sensitive canine ear.

"Let's get you set-up," Wash went on with a purr. His paw left Drake's chest and moved up the wolfox's arms. Drake felt pressure on his wrists, and he looked up to see the raccoon attaching a pair of cuffs, leaving him shackled to the sonic shower's emitter. The instant the cuffs clicked, Drake's heart started pounding. *Fuck. Fuck. Fuck.* Every concern came back: Drake knew how things needed to work—which was why he took charge. But giving it up? He didn't know if he could.

The wolfox tugged at the cuffs in a move that he prayed looked like checking to see if they were secure while Wash's paws wandered down his sides. The raccoon said something, but the words were lost in the hammering of the wolfox's heartbeat. A whimper escaped Drake's muzzle. *I can't do this!*

Get it together! You've posed with cuffs before. He was there for those.

Yeah, but this is different. What am I going to do if I don't like it?

Tell him!

But he's lead!

Drake tried to keep the struggle internal—but with Wash leaning against him, the raccoon noticed the wolfox tense up.

"Yellow?" he asked. "Or red?" The raccoon's arm left him and reached up to the cuffs.

"Yellow!" Drake bit out, making an effort not to shout.

Wash's weight lifted off of the wolfox. Opening his eyes, Drake saw that his boyfriend was still holding his paw over the cuffs' quick-release. Drake slumped to his knees, and the raccoon followed him down.

"Fuck that. You're red, hun. I'm getting you out of these. I'm sorry—"

"No!" Drake growled. "Yellow."

"What do you need, babe? Tell me. No bullshit. Tell me."

The commander's mind raced, running through possibility after possibility. He knew Wash wouldn't judge him if he couldn't go through with it, but something in him didn't want to quit. He reached a decision in an instant.

"I need a minute," he replied, his breathing steadying.

"Okay," Wash said, rubbing his back. They'd established that Drake wanted his "minutes" alone, but the raccoon was reluctant to allow that. "I'm going to check the locker room real quick. Do you want me to undo the cuffs?"

"No."

"Are you sure? Don't lie."

Drake took a steadying breath. "Leave them on."

Leaning against the bulkhead, Drake pulled himself upright. Wash assisted with a supporting paw under his boyfriend's arms before leaving the stall. Drake, lost in his own thoughts, barely noticed him leave. *Why the fuck can't I do this?* It was so simple: just literally do nothing, let Wash take charge while he became a pup. Well, that was an overstatement—but it was the general concept.

Never be afraid of something you like, Silver's voice cut into his thoughts. She would know, of course. She and Crimson often engaged in pup play, and she'd invited him to join in some scenes back before Drake had met his boyfriend. He knew the vixen had been the one to suggest that kind of play to Wash— including having the raccoon take charge. In the last scene Drake had done with the foxes, Silver had gotten him to let go for just a moment…and when the wolfox realized what happened, he'd left mid-scene when he realized he was obeying Silver without even thinking about it, and never played with them since.

"Fuck," he whispered.

The self-doubts and fears of the unknown hammered at him, threatening to drive him back to his knees. Even as he struggled with them, a new thought occurred to him: he was shackled to the wall of a public shower. He would look like a prank victim, and of one of the oldest ones in the book. That wouldn't do for the Starfighter Wing Commander. Granted, only Crimson and Silver were supposed to use this shower—but he knew it was only a matter of time before someone else came in. Why had Wash insisted on doing this in public? Wasn't asking someone who'd maintained control for a decade to give it up a big enough hurdle to get over? But something in him wouldn't say no.

He felt a paw on his side.

"Still yellow?" Wash asked as he caressed the line where Drake's reddish-brown fur met his cream belly fur.

"I wish we weren't doing this in public," the wolfox replied with a whimper.

"This isn't public, Foxy," the raccoon soothed as he massaged his boyfriend's back. "It was already cleaned today, so the only people that would come in are Silver and Crimson—the worst they'd do is join in."

"You know other people *could* come."

"Okay," Wash said, his paws leaving Drake's back. "Why don't we get you cleaned up? You need it. If you're still yellow after that, we'll call it off. Fair?"

Drake thought about it, deciding it would give them a chance to try playing with Wash in charge but would be over quickly if Drake wasn't up to it. He nodded.

"Ok," Wash said as he reached up to turn the shower on. Drake gave the raccoon's cheek ruff a lick to show he was trying to be in the mood. Wash giggled, returned the lick and continued, keeping his nose against the wolfox's cheek as he reached for the soap. Then with much kissing, nuzzling, groping, and fondling, the raccoon lathered and cleaned his mate's fur.

Much attention was paid to Drake's cheek ruffs, his sensitive ears, and then down to his hips. The soap that the wolfox favored was just enough to take the edge off his stronger canine musk, meaning that he could smell the raccoon's scent as Wash pressed close—the pine of the soap adding a slightly exotic feel to the whole experience. Drake forced himself to take deep breaths and focused on the shower wall. The fears didn't go away, but his heartbeat had slowed a little. In his loins, he felt a familiar stirring. *I don't know if I want that right now.*

"Well now," Wash chuckled as his soapy paws came around Drake's hips and found the wolfox's feelings on the experience. "Someone's actually enjoying this."

"I always enjoy time with you," Drake said through chattering teeth as the raccoon began to soap his sheath, sack, and the tip of his shaft that was already emerging.

"Oh, it's not that bad, is it?" Wash asked as he spread the soap over Drake's hips and down his muscular rump and under his fluffy tail.

"I've been worse," Drake admitted after a moment of reflection.

"Still yellow?"

"Getting better."

"Okay." Wash spread his boyfriend's firm, well-rounded cheeks and gently ran his paws over them. Drake moaned in spite of himself, then gasped as Wash's cock poked the wolfox right under his rump. The earthy, spiced wood scent of raccoon overpowered the smell of soap.

Drake breathed in the raccoon's musk, letting it arouse him even more as Wash backed up then knelt to soap up his thighs. *Fuck, this is actually kind of hot. Is he getting everywhere? I wish I could check. No! Cut it out! Just try and let him have his fun.*

Meanwhile, Wash knelt down to scrub the wolfox's socks, an action that brought the raccoon's nose directly behind the canine's sack. Drake bit back a half howl as the warm breath passed over his balls. He could smell his own arousal, woody like the oak forest back on Terra, mingling with Wash's.

The raccoon chuckled and bit the tail smacking his face as he cleaned the commander's paws, holding it in his muzzle. Drake let out a yip, surprised that he was wagging more than by the playful bite itself.

Goddamnit, get yourself together. You know he's going to take that as you're enjoying this.

I... think I am?

That *much?*

I don't know! I wish he'd hurry. I should tell him to hurry.

Wash let go of his mate's tail and stood up. The raccoon

sniffed, the usual clue that he was thinking.

Wash's presence left Drake, and the wolfox's doubts, quieted by the close contact with his boyfriend, came screaming back. He whimpered and tugged on the cuffs. A comforting chitter brought his focus back outside his head.

"Over here, Pet. Focus on Sir."

Drake's ears drooped at the terms, but looked over his right arm to find Wash standing there, holding the soap to the lighter gray chest fur of his chest. He favored the wolfox with that devious smile that raccoons did so well and proceeded to lather himself up, as he'd done to his mate a moment before. He started with his ears, worked his way through his cheek ruffs, and cleaned his mask and narrower muzzle before dropping his paws to his well-muscled chest.

Wash purred and worked his way down his almost monochromatic-gray body, though he took considerable time on his exposed pink shaft and gray sack. Despite his efforts to maintain composure, Drake found himself wagging. The raccoon chuckled and turned his back to the wolfox and cleaned his bushy rigged tail before lifting it to massage suds into his rear. Drake huffed as he felt his shaft throb. He tugged on the cuffs again. *Ringtail. We need to go!*

Wash snickered as he put the soap back on the shelf. Drake leaned out to whisper at Wash to hurry, but the raccoon pressed his nose against the wolfox's cheek and pushed him away.

"Down boy," Wash whispered into his boyfriend's ear before giving it a nip. "You took a long time in the lav before you came in the shower. Were you a good fox pup and got yourself ready?"

"But we need to go," Drake growled.

"None of that, Pet. Relax, and answer Sir's question. With words."

"Yes, *Sir*," Drake replied with an exasperated sigh. "All ready. Lubed and everythin—"

His reply was changed to a moan as Wash squeezed his rear with one paw and gently inserted a finger into Drake's prepared hole. The wolfox groaned and wiggled as Wash worked another digit in and swirled them around. After another moment, he withdrew his fingers and kissed Drake's cheek. Over the hum of the shower, he heard the click of a bottle opening.

"Good boy," the raccoon whispered. He reached down and lifted Drake's left leg, then positioned the tip of his shaft right against the wolfox's rear. He gently wiggled his hips to rub his head over the sensitive opening. "Always so thoughtful. Ready, Pet?"

Drake thought about stopping him, calling it off. But he admitted to himself that at least on some level, he was sort of enjoying this—if the almost painful erection he was sporting was anything to go by. Silver had said he would. Had he been thinking about it wrong? Maybe instead of worrying about not being in control he should just focus on being the center of attention. *He...Sir...still needs to hurry the hell up though. Fuck.*

Drake nodded and yapped, shoving back against the raccoon, staggering him a step. Wash took the hint, aligned himself, and pressed forward—sliding into Drake's waiting entrance with a smooth motion. The wolfox gasped and moaned loudly as the shaft slid inside him. The electric tingle of being penetrated shot through his spine, up to his ears and down to the tip of his tail. He groaned and pulled at the cuffs as he felt himself instinctively clench against Wash's shaft. That elicited a purr from the raccoon as he began to thrust into the wolfox.

Wash set a rapid pace while the canine remained cuffed to the shower with a leg in the air. Drake moaned and whimpered, with the occasional growl. He tried to enjoy the feeling of having a thick raccoon shaft inside him, but the need to be quick kept the pleasure moderate. He kept pushing back against his lover, trying to keep the pace up. *Faster. Com'on!*

"Stop." The single growled word caused the wolfox to freeze.

He stared at the wall as the warmth of raccoon shaft slid out of him. Drake whimpered as it hit him that he'd messed up. *Oh shit...*

"Pet." The word somehow focused his attention. "Let Sir take care of you."

Drake bit his lip. He took a deep breath and focused. *Try. Be a good pup. Be a good pup. You take care of Sir, let Sir take care of Pet...*

The last thought, coming out of almost nowhere, brought the fighter pilot's mind to a halt. He latched onto it and let it fill him. Then the revelation hit him hard enough that his conscious mind didn't register Wash reentering his rear. It was about being partners in all things. As the commanding officer, he was in control of almost every aspect of their lives—was it too much to let the raccoon take charge in the bedroom? To let go, just a little.

His body relaxed. No other words came, just a fuzzy void in his head that was focused solely on the pleasure of a raccoon sliding back and forth inside him. The commander, the pilot, the mate that worried about his relationship were all gone. There was only Pet being taken care of by Sir. His tongue lolled out of his mouth, and he let out a moaning sigh. He felt the pressure build inside as Wash chittered and took Drake's scruff in his muzzle. The wolfox panted as the raccoon picked up his pace even more and took a tighter grip on Drake's hips. Wash growled into his mate's neck, setting an even faster pace. Drake sighed in contentment, the panting on his neck a sign that Wash was on the final approach.

With one last thrust, the raccoon hilted the wolfox, and Drake felt the shaft inside him spasm as Wash released his seed into his mate. The raccoon shuddered and collapsed against Drake as he came down from his orgasm. He panted and nuzzled his lover while the wolfox shook his head. Wash chuckled and slid out.

"Good Pet," the raccoon said, patting the wolfox on the rear. "Now, don't spill any."

Drake nodded and squeezed his cheeks tight to comply with the request as Wash reached up and hit the quick release on the cuffs. The euphoric haze of pup headspace fading, Drake realized that he still had a "problem." He whimpered and wiggled his hips to wave his untouched erection in the fading mist.

"Don't worry, Pet. We'll take care of that, I promise," Wash soothed as he turned off the shower. "Just not here. Why don't you walk out?"

The wolfox nodded and, with the cuffs still attached to his left wrist, waddled out into the locker room shuddering slightly as he went through the fur drying station. *Holy shit. I did it! I was a good pet... but damnit, Sir was reckless about it. Can I really trust Sir if this was his idea of a first time?*

They reached the locker room, and Drake saw what Wash had in mind: laid out on the bench, beside two towels, was a collection of items that could loosely be called clothing. Next to those was one of their prized self-lubricating butt plugs.

"What the *fuck*?" Drake all but shouted. The good will of the shower was gone. "Wash? What the fuck are you thinking having all this out in plain sight?"

"Relax, fox. And I didn't say you could use words."

"No! Don't 'fox' me," Drake growled as he wheeled around to face Wash. "Sex in the shower is one thing, exposing our private lives for everyone to see is something else. I'm not playing this game with someone I can't trust."

"But you can trust me," Wash muttered after a moment of silence. "Look at the door."

Drake turned again, teeth bared, but the snarl died as his eyes focused on what the raccoon was talking about: hanging across the controls was a lock scrambler. Drake blinked as a rush of emotions hit him all at once. Wash hadn't been reckless; he'd thought it out and planned to make sure Drake was as comfortable as possible. Relief overwhelmed the anger and the tension. He sighed and began to tremble. But one emotion didn't quite leave him.

"You should have told me," Drake said. He turned back to Wash, clenching his rear again as he remembered that if he didn't they'd have to go back into the shower.

"I did tell you," Wash admitted. "Right when I put the cuffs on. Didn't you hear me? I thought you were role playing."

Drake wanted to launch into an argument about making sure things were heard, but it died almost instantly. He had no backup here and knew the only ones he could try would be on Wash's side. The urge to say he was done returned, but it found no traction. At every turn, Wash had put Drake's comfort first and foremost, even if he hadn't exactly told Drake that he had. The part of him that felt he needed to be in charge was growing quiet. He still didn't fully understand why he was afraid of letting go, but he wasn't going to let it rule him anymore. *I've gone this far. Might as well keep the flight going.*

"So," he sighed, feeling the warm fuzziness begin to fill him again. "What now?"

"Well. Uh." Wash scratched behind his ear. "I was gonna get you geared up, and then was gonna walk you back to our quarters on a leash…"

Drake cocked his head and favored Wash with the glare he reserved for pilots that crashed doing stunts on approach to landing. The raccoon flinched and scrambled for the datapad sitting on the bench, his tail flicking behind him.

"I know, I know. Big step. But I thought of that. Look." He typed something in and then held it up for the wolfox to see the text conversation.

Got it. Will make sure its all clear.

Thx!

Hey! We're comin out in a minute. Still good?

An ellipsis appeared at the bottom of the screen, flashed, and then was replaced by a new line of text. *All clear. Got 15 min of empty corridors. ;3*

Drake stared at the screen and sighed. "You told her."

"Well, who else could I get help from and not have you pitch a fit?" Wash snorted and chittered.

"I'm going yellow again…"

"Come on, ace." Wash flashed a big smile. His tail swished behind him. "Think of it as an opportunity to show off. But I've got your robe if you go red."

Drake crossed his arms and huffed as his tail flicked behind him. His attempt at annoyance was undone by his erection, which throbbed and released a spurt of pre.

"That's one advantage I have over them—I've learned what makes you tick."

Drake sighed, his ears going flat. He shook his head and barked in acceptance before the raccoon could reply.

Wash nodded and reached for the plug, giving it a squeeze to let the lube begin to seep through its surface from the internal reservoir. That done, he activated the vibrating feature and slipped it under Drake's tail. Drake swore and whimpered as the vibrations began to stimulate his insides, making his cock twitch.

The wolfox's erection, which had flagged a little during their argument shot back to full hardness, his knot rapidly swelling. Drake panted but felt the vibrations ease, backing him away from an impending climax. He took a step forward and braced himself against the bench, his reddish-pink shaft throbbing in time with the plug's hums. Wash chuckled and set the remote down before kissing the canine on the cheek.

"Let's get you dressed, shall we?" he asked with a naughty smile.

Dressed was something of an overstatement as Drake looked at the items on the bench. One form-fitting black jockstrap that was Wash's favorite in the wolfox's collection, one black leather collar with ring and a leash sitting next to it, and one leather pup hood that looked like a "sexy" imitation of a fighter pilot's helmet. It was cut so that it would sit on the top of the head, covering halfway down the wearer's muzzle and cheeks, as well as the front of their ears. A series of snaps around the eye cutouts hinted that the raccoon had removed something from the hood. Drake let out a questioning whine.

"What better fantasy is there than having a soldier pup to take care of? Also, it came with blinders, but I figured we weren't ready for those."

Drake squinted at it, then tapped the emblem on it, and then pointed at Sir.

"Well what the hell else was it gonna be?" Wash asked with a swish and a smirk. "Shall we hurry?"

Out of the corner of his eye, Drake saw the raccoon pull on a set of formfitting boxer briefs and then look over at the wolfox with concern as his practiced fingers fastened the waistband over his tail.

Drake's nose twitched a little and then let out a little sigh. He tapped his muzzle, the agreed-on sign that he was asking to use words. "The hood has fasteners along the muzzle. We using those?"

"Yeah, they keep it on better when moving around a lot."

"How am I supposed to eject if I can't vocalize?" the wolfox asked.

"By pulling the cord," the raccoon replied. "Like in the days before voice commands."

He reached behind the robes on the bench and produced a black circle slightly smaller than the raccoon's paw with a notch cut in it: a portable signal light. Wash blinked out a pattern—*I love you*. Then the raccoon hugged his mate and held him tight and gently rubbed their muzzles against each other's. The whole scene might have been cute and romantic to an observer—except for the wolfox's leaking erection and the buzzing coming from under his tail.

"Okay," Drake said with a lick to Wash's muzzle. "We can do this."

Wash fully understood what the words meant, if the broad smile on his muzzle was anything to go by.

Drake reached out and took the jockstrap and put it on. It took a couple tries—once, he dropped the jock when a particularly good vibration gave him a full body shudder. He managed, but the outline of his erection was clearly visible under the stretchy fabric pressed up against his groin. Almost immediately, a wet spot formed at the tip of the tent. Wash giggled as Drake's shaft throbbed in its fabric confines before leaning in and kissing him on the cheek. He pulled the wolfox's arms behind him and cuffed his wrists again.

"Good?" The raccoon asked as he placed the signal light in Drake's paw.

The wolfox squeezed it and blinked out *Okay*. Wash nodded and positioned the hood on Drake.

"Why's the back of this open?" Drake asked as it settled into place. "That's not very realistic."

The answer came as Wash scratched behind the wolfox's ears. Drake let out an involuntary *ahoo* of pleasure, drawing a chuckle from the raccoon. Wash looked for a final confirmation from the canine then secured the fasteners under Drake's muzzle. Drake worked his mouth open and shut a few times: he could vocalize if he needed to, and breathe comfortably, but speaking was out. *Drives home that Pet doesn't talk.* Wash waited for a confirming nod before fastening the collar on Drake and attaching the leash. Then the raccoon slipped on his robe and took the leash in one paw tucking Drake's robe under his arm.

With his mate in tow, Wash went to the door, undid the scrambler, and stuck his head out into the corridor. *We're actually doing this.* Drake instinctively tried to sniff, but it was useless—all he could smell was the leather of the hood and the woody scent of his own arousal. The wolfox twitched as Wash ducked his head back in.

"All clear. You doing okay, Pet?"

Drake whimpered and turned as much as the leash would allow. *Getting warm back here, Sir,* he blinked.

"How warm?" Wash asked, sudden concern on his face as he fished in his pocket for the controller. The vibrations eased and there was a slight cooling sensation in his insides as the plug released more lube. "Better? You need me to turn it off?"

Okay now, Drake blinked, letting out a relieved sigh.

With a gentle tug, Wash pulled Drake into the deserted corridor. Despite the appearances, the wolfox's ears kept twitching and his head was on a swivel. His heart was racing again as the fear of getting caught hammered at him. And yet... There was an element of fun. His tail swished behind him as they walked. *I...Pet... can do this.*

It didn't remain deserted for long. As they rounded the one corner between the locker room and their quarters, Sir slowed. Drake came around the bend to see Silver and Crimson standing in the corridor, their backs to opposite bulkheads as if they had been chatting. He sighed internally—so much for the faint hope that Silver would be content with just knowing he'd tried letting go.

The two foxes looked up as Sir approached with Drake in tow. Silver's smile was that of a proud teacher as she looked on at her students before trotting down the corridor to give Wash a hug. Crimson gave Drake the sympathetic smile of someone who'd been in similar situations. Silver finished her hug with the raccoon and then looked Drake over.

"Well look at you," the vixen said with a purr. She turned back to her other student. "May I inspect the pup?"

She waited for the nod of agreement to pass between them, then took the leash from Sir and walked around Drake. "I'm really liking this look for you, Commander. Or is it Pet?"

"Pet," Sir replied.

"And you were so freaked out when I called you that," Silver said with a laugh. "Love that jockstrap. Crim? Do I have one of those for you?"

"I don't think so," the reddish-orange reynard replied after giving Drake's garment a quick glance. "But black wouldn't look as good on me. All my gear is green."

"Hmm," Silver mused as she studied Drake's crotch.

The wolfox's sense of modesty returned, provoking him to flinch and turn away. A sharp tug on the leash stopped him.

"No need for that, Pet," Silver cooed, but Drake could hear the steel just under the comforting tone. "I've already seen how big your knot is."

"Should have felt it," Crimson added with a smirk.

"I was going to," Silver said.

Drake winced as she paused, worried she was going to complete the story.

Silver just smiled. "Maybe once Pet is more comfortable as a pup, I will some time."

Drake's glanced over at Wash, making sure the vixen saw.

"Of course," she soothed. "I wouldn't dream of it without your Sir." She leaned a little closer to the wolfox, though she spoke loud enough for them all to hear "It's easier with him, isn't it? With us it was just a game you didn't understand. With your Sir, it's love."

The wolfox considered that for a moment. Something in the words rang true with him: it had been easier to let go with Wash. Silver had only gotten him there when he was on the edge of orgasm, in the shower and somewhat here, he'd managed long before that. He nodded.

"They did have them in green," Wash put in, pulling back to the previous topic. "I can send you the catalog."

"Thank you," Silver said. She walked closer to Drake. "May I touch?"

Wash looked at Drake and got a nod from the wolfox. "It's okay."

Silver also looked for the nod but waited for the raccoon's reply before she reached down and put a black furred paw on Drake's hip. She grinned as she felt the vibrations from the plug through the wolfox's body.

"Very nice," she purred. "What is that? The DomPlug V2?"

"The V3," Wash said with a smile. "It's got custom programmable vibration settings. There's a sensor ring in the lube chamber which can record your style of topping."

"Oh, you naughty raccoon," Silver cooed. "Is he fucking himself?"

Suddenly, the vibrations in his rear changed and Drake let out a half whimper, half howl in response.

"He is now," Wash replied with a grin. "With the lube reservoir and the pressure sensor, the plug can edge you for three hours."

"Safely?" Silver asked as she removed her paw from Drake's hip and looked sternly at Wash.

"We haven't tried it that long," the raccoon replied with a swish of his tail. "Not going to right now either. Probably needs some adjusting to the vibrations—he was complaining about it getting warm a few minutes ago. Turning down the vibrations and releasing some more lube helped that."

"Not good," Silver mused. "Pet's okay now? Oh, a signal light. Clever. Okay, good. Still, probably best for you boys to get moving."

She reached up and gave Drake a scratch behind his ears. The wolfox purred in appreciation. Silver patted him on the rear before handing the leash back to Wash and whispering something Drake couldn't quite catch. He could guess though: Silver was protective of him, especially as he was exploring the more giving aspects of his relationship with Wash. From the look on Wash's face, Silver had both praised him and given him a stern reminder. Drake resisted the urge to flinch again—he couldn't help but see the reprimand as his fault. But he had to let it go, to let Wash take the responsibility.

Drake and Sir continued on, and Crimson threw the pair a salute as they passed. Drake wagged, and they reached their quarters without any further incident. Wash led him to the foot of their bed, undid the cuffs, and then went and locked the door. The wolfox remained standing where his mate had stopped him with his paws up to his collar like a good pup was supposed to. He had to admit he actually felt rather sexy being a pup. It was kind of freeing in a way.

He had barely contemplated that when he was knocked off his paws and slammed onto the bed, with the weight of a fully grown raccoon pinning him down. Sir leaned back, allowing Drake to roll over before the raccoon was kissing and nuzzling him with an energy that bordered on desperation. Paws worked their way up Drake's chest and neck before finding the hood clasps under his muzzle before moving behind his head. The hood came off, and a nuzzle was pushed into his ear.

"Oh Foxy," Wash breathed in a husky tone. "You were perfect. You were so sexy."

A warm wet pressure pushed against the inside of Drake's ear as the raccoon licked it hungrily and sent shivers through the wolfox. Drake moaned at the attention, but some part of him was confused by not being called "Pet." He looked past the raccoon's shoulder. Drake could see that his boyfriend was completely naked and if the sensation poking him in the stomach was anything to go by, he was also fully erect. Wash turned his attention to Drake's other ear.

"God, Drake, it was all I could do to keep my paws off you. I love you, baby. So much."

With Wash's tongue buried in his ear, Drake could only moan in reply. He reached down to show he was a good pet by stroking the raccoon's shaft, but Wash took hold of his wrist.

"Don't worry about that," the raccoon said lustily as he

reached up to undo Drake's collar.

The wolfox put his paws up to block the move. Wash leaned back in surprise, a puzzled frown on his muzzle. His ear twitched, and Drake let out a whimper as his own ears folded down. Wash laughed.

"That's right. I'm sorry," he caressed his boyfriend's chest. "It's okay. Pet and Sir Time is over. Now is all you. You let me have my fun. Now we take care of you. Tell me what you want to do. We'll do *anything* you want."

The wolfox thought about that for a moment, and finally dropped his paws away from his neck. Wash reached behind his mate's neck and undid the fastening. Drake felt…something almost like loss…as the pressure left his throat, while Wash leaned back and removed Drake's soaked jockstrap. The wolfox looked up to see the fur on Wash's torso matted down with his own pre. The raccoon's shaft bobbed invitingly in front of him, which caused Drake to run his tongue over his muzzle. The raccoon smiled, but remained where he was, clearly waiting for Drake to make the next move.

It didn't take long for Drake to decide on something. *It might not be Pet and Sir Time, but he can still be in charge.* A moment later, the wolfox reached up and pulled him into a tight hug. As they held each other, Drake whispered into Wash's ear before giving it a playful nip. Wash giggled.

"That's going to get you in the shower again. You are so dirty sometimes."

"*All* the times," Drake replied deadpan.

"One more reason I love you," Wash said with a kiss.

For a minute, the two lovers kissed and nuzzled each other, licking muzzles, nipping ears, and rubbing their erections together. Moans, groans, and giggles escaped from the pair. Wash gave Drake a quick kiss to his cheek ruff, then lifted himself off the canine. He left the bed and began to rummage for something in the nightstand drawer. Drake took advantage of the situation, reaching over to caress the raccoon's muscular rump with his paw. Wash lifted his tail helpfully to give Drake full access while he continued to work with something in the drawer. Soon, the raccoon returned to the bed, the mate of the plug inside Drake in his paws. A moment later, Wash pressed the lubricated plug into his own rear with a gasp as it slid inside. The raccoon leaned to the side and entered a command into the controls for both plugs. The wolfox moaned and whimpered as it registered that Wash had set the vibration to the raccoon's own thrusting pattern.

The raccoon smiled and groaned himself as he straddled Drake's thighs, letting their shafts touch and vibrate. They sat there and rubbed each other's hips as they reveled in the sense of being fucked by their mate even though their cocks were lying against each other's. Drake's knot began to swell again as the wolfox moved his paw to stroke his boyfriend. He was rewarded with hearing the raccoon's own whimpers of pleasure. Wash leaned down and spent the next few moments running his paws up and down Drake's sides and nuzzling, chittering, and groaning into Drake's sensitive ears. It didn't take long for the wolfox to begin moaning in return as he began to feel the pressure of an orgasm building in his loins.

Wash apparently wasn't far behind, as he reached down and pulled Drake's paw from his shaft as he pulled himself up to a sitting position. The raccoon reached down and took hold of both their cocks, which had been leaking enough pre for lubrication as Wash stroked them. It didn't take long for them to begin to moan and pant as orgasms built inside them. Drake pushed his hips up against Wash as the raccoon picked up his pace. The feeling was electric, and the wolfox shuddered and sensed his mate shake as well.

A moment later, both of them let out loud moans as their heads rolled back in pleasure. Wash pointed their cocks at his lover a moment before his shaft throbbed in release. Drake was right behind him, letting out a low howl as the pressure in his loins finally exploded. He felt splashes of warmth against his fur, coating him in a line from his groin, up his torso, and hitting the underside of his chin.

They panted through their shared ecstasy, shafts twitching against each other as they released several pulses on to Drake's fur. The wolfox reveled in the sensation as he came shuddering and panting down from the heights of his climax. The exhausted raccoon flopped onto his mate, and for several minutes they just lay there and cuddled. Wash reached over and switched the plugs off before they dozed in each other's arms.

Drake woke ten minutes later. Carefully, the wolfox pulled his arm out from under the still sleeping raccoon, but he wasn't careful enough, and Wash's gold eyes opened.

"So soon?" he asked sleepily.

"Just for a few minutes, Ringtail. We need to get cleaned up and then we can get some real sleep," Drake reassured him as he got to his paws and pulled his plug out. One of the perks of Drake's rank was that his quarters did have a shower stall—but it was just barely large enough for one of them to shower alone, which was why it went unused in most circumstances. "At least for an hour or so."

"Aww, why?"

"You know why, hun. I gotta check on the second patrol when they get back."

"Okay," Wash said in the tone of someone who didn't like an answer but decided they weren't going to fight it. Getting Drake to let go in the bedroom was a big enough victory for the day. He ran a paw through his mate's matted belly fur, then pulled his own plug out and put it in the canine's outstretched paw. "Use the honey lemon soap, it's the best at getting rid of the sex smell without being obvious that that's what you're doing."

"Yes dear," Drake replied and headed to the shower with a happy wag.

Drake looked back as he entered the lav to see Wash watching him go. As the wolfox turned away, he saw a smile play across the raccoon's lips. It wasn't until he set the plugs on the sink that he realized what Wash had been smiling at: he'd picked up the collar with the toys. A smile of his own appeared in the mirror. *Yeah. I could get used to this. And it does look nice. Maybe Pet will wear it more often...*

The Competition

Thomas "Faux" Steele

Princess

"Have you decided yet, sweetheart?" The bartender, a busty cheetah with claws painted shocking pink, stands expectantly behind the stainless-steel countertop. She pours me another coffee and tops it with whipped cream and a dash of nutmeg. Off to the side, the honky-tonk pianist belts out a traditional Scottish ode to a bull with five cocks.

"Could I get another minute? This is a lot to take in." I hide my muzzle behind the smooth leather menu, my nails digging into the embossed paper.

"Sure thing, sugar. I see you have the all-inclusive package, so if there's anything you'd like to try, just give me a holler." She turns and heads down the bar, retrieving a length of red silk rope from underneath before making a beeline for the red panda at a corner table.

The menu of services is intimidating. I nervously flip through it, my eyes glossing over line-after-line of experiences. I skip over the section labeled "hardcore" entirely. I decide to stay in the first area of the menu, where things seem to be a little tamer. My eyes pause on item sixty-six. It's labeled simply "kitten." Unlike some of the other items, there's no description beneath it. It seems an innocent enough place to start.

When my girlfriend, Bella, convinced me to take a trip down to the Isla del Placer, I figured our vacation would involve a few seminars with some exotic equipment and plenty of time catching rays on the beach. I've dipped my toes in kink before, even gone to a few meet-ups, but this is on another level. Heading down to a full piano bar with an assortment of kinks on tap is definitely not how I expected I'd be spending my first afternoon.

"Have you made up your mind?" A tall wolf with flint grey eyes leans over me. Like the other employees, he's immaculately dressed in black-tie formal, though his clothes are tailored tight enough that they don't hide his muscular form. Everyone who works here exudes a calming, stoic energy, and while it's a little unnerving at first, it does make it easier to be confident in my decision.

"Could I get the kitten, please?" I whisper, and then violently slam the menu shut, my ears folding in embarrassment.

"An excellent choice, kitten." The wolf reaches under the counter and assembles a kinky spread for my inspection. Bright pink lacy panties with "PRINCESS" embroidered across the crotch. A dainty pink collar with a bright silver bell suspended from the D-ring. A faux fur tail sleeve with an orange and black calico pattern and matching ear prostheses.

"The panties are a nice touch." Bella went through the concierge on her platinum card, so I can see why they don't spare any expense. She wanted to do something to spice up our sex life. Perhaps this might be just what the doctor ordered.

"Of course. I think they suit you." He gathers the outfit and motions for me to follow him. We go past a table where two hyenas are chowing down on a zebra carcass. I cock an eyebrow. "Simulated vore with lab-grown meat. I've been told it tastes just like the real thing."

He takes me through a lightweight velvet curtain into a sterile, dimly-lit hallway. Identical doors jut out from the polished marble every ten feet, each marked with an antiqued bronze number plate. I take a few deep inhales, but the air doesn't reveal any secrets. The low grumble of an air purifier drowns out any ambient sounds quieter than the steady sound of our footsteps. We turn a corner, and the wolf halts in front of door sixty-six.

The lock clicks and the door slides inward. The lights come on slowly, staying dimmed low enough that my corneas aren't seared by the LEDs. A cat bed big enough for several adults to curl up comfortably in is set against the far wall. Paddles and other spanking implements dangle from stainless steel hooks above it. The walls are lined with metal shelving holding a variety of toys and accessories. A faintly minty scent permeates the room.

"So, what does kitten play involve? I'm a little new to the kink scene, and I thought I'd use this vacation to broaden my horizons." I stand around awkwardly with my arms crossed, taking it all in.

The wolf shoots me a soft smile as the door swings shut. He straightens his bowtie and gently pats the bed. "Like any kink play, there's no right way to do it. Let's get you properly outfitted and go from there. Sound good to you?"

I flop down on the bed, nervously pitter-pattering my hooves on the floor. "Sure, you're the expert here."

The wolf's paws are gentle as he slides my jeans and panties down. "I'm not an expert, I'm more of a…sexual tour guide," he mutters, gesturing for me to raise my arms. "After a while of working here, you end up knowing a little about everything."

"You've done this before, right?" He peels my tank top off, his perfectly-manicured nails brushing against my topcoat. Unhooking my bra, he replaces it with something with more support.

"Once or twice." The tail and ears are the easy part. They simply slide over my existing appendages, making me a little fuzzier than I naturally am. I take a deep breath and close my eyes as he playfully slides my panties up. He steps back to examine his work as I lazily sprawl out on the cat bed. "I find the kitten headspace harder to define than that of a pup or a pony, but what I'd advise is approaching it through the lens of reducing your inhibitions. Think like a kitten would, and I'll do my best to reward that behavior."

"Okay!" I shoot him an eager smile and then arch my back, holding the position for a few moments until I feel the tension ease.

"Good kitten! Just like that." He fishes around in his front pocket for a moment before whipping a gummy shark onto the bed. My favorite. I wriggle my bottom for a moment before eagerly snapping it up. It's sweet and vaguely fruity, bringing back warm foalhood memories of filling a little plastic bag with anything I wanted at the candy store in the mall every Friday.

"Do you have a name you'd like be called, while you're in kitten space?" The wolf leans over and tinkles the bell around my neck before heading into the kitchenette.

Glassware clinks, and the fridge pops open. "Princess, if that's alright."

"I think that's a perfect name for a kitten. Princess it is. Now, drink up. Kittens need their milk." The wolf places a gold-rimmed saucer on the floor. My stomach grumbles at me, and I realize I chose sleep over going down to one of the hotel restaurants to grab something for lunch. Time to embrace the kitten life. I drop down to my paws and knees, lapping the milk up with my large equine tongue. It's oddly relaxing. The wolf sits on the bed and tenderly runs his paw through my mane as I drink.

"And what's your name?" I pause my lapping to let him pour more milk from a tall glass bottle.

"Bacchus. All staff are named after Roman gods, if that makes it easier to remember." He scritches behind my right ear, making me thump my hooves in pleasure. The milk is supremely creamy and surprisingly filling. After finishing the last dregs, I lean back and purr softly in contentment. "But you can also call me whatever dominant term you're most comfortable with."

"Okay, Master." I lean into his paw as he gently wipes my muzzle with a handkerchief.

"See? Was that really so bad?" I shake my head as he plops down next to me on the deep-pile carpet. I claim his lap as my own, allowing him to calmly run his paw down the length of my spine as he leans back against the bed. "It's nice to be a kitten, isn't it, Princess?"

Another gummy shark slides into my muzzle. I contentedly

chew on it as Bacchus teases my tail, his paw darting around as I try and slam my rear tuft down on it. I focus on the vibration of his paw in the air, sensing motion through my unconscious animal instincts. After a few fruitless minutes, I finally slam the tip of my tail down on his wrist. Victory. I dial up the volume of my purring, gently nuzzling my cheek against his pant leg.

"Such a smart girl." He gestures towards the door with his free paw. "You know, if you'd like to show off your kitten skills for a crowd, there's a competition happening in a little while. Does that sound like something you'd enjoy, Princess?"

I nod, my eyes going wide as the crystal set in the chunky silver ring on his index claw suddenly fills with light, glowing with the brilliance of a star. A holographic calendar stretches out nearly to the ceiling, neon-colored boxes showing the events for the afternoon. One near the top flashes bright pink before the projection vanishes. "The top prize is a complimentary stay for two here at the Isla del Placer, so Master hopes you'll do your best. I'm sure Bella would appreciate it."

His stoic energy flows into me as he holds me close, a strong arm wrapped around me. His scent is pungent and masculine, but it doesn't smell quite like domestic canine. It's more like dog with a wild edge, a rich, earthy undertone like freshly-dug truffles. "Let me know when you're ready to go, kitten. We'll take things at your pace."

He climbs to his feet with a grunt of effort and moves toward the door. I follow behind him for a few paces, then sneakily go right into the kitchen. I've barely finished wrapping my hands around the bag of gummy sharks left open on the counter before I feel a tug on my collar.

"Looks like someone just earned themselves a leashing." I whine loudly as my prize spills onto the granite. Master drags me back into the play area collar-first, giving me little opportunity to resist. From among the other pieces of gear, he snatches a neon pink leash studded with rhinestones. He attaches it to the ring around my collar and gives it a light tug. "Now, let's get going, kitten. We wouldn't want to be late to the festivities."

We head further down the hallway, the numbers on the

doors continuing to climb. I follow Master's lead, though I occasionally pause to explore when I manage to catch an interesting sensation on our way. I catch a strong whiff of baby powder from one door, and explore subtle scorch marks on the threshold of another, rubbing it until the carbon darkens my pawpads. Master indulges me, letting me enjoy myself until we reach the elevator. The door contrasts with the austerity of the hallway with its art deco mosaic of Zeus' abduction of Ganymede. It slides open as we approach. I squat on my haunches as I enter, purring softly as he strokes through my mane.

The elevator whizzes upwards for a few moments before abruptly coming to a halt. Bacchus glances at his digital watch before giving a playful tug on my leash. "Shall we, kitten?"

I put up a token resistance, but the wolf is nothing if not steadfast. I eventually relent, allowing him to lead me through another long hallway, this one more brightly lit. I recognize it from earlier as part the conference center. Electronic panels next to the oak double doors display what activities are on offer inside. I spot a fox blowing up a balloon on one before Bacchus pulls me through a brass-lined archway. We emerge into a grand ballroom, dozens of spectators lining the tiered platforms around the center stage. The other two competitors, a pup and a pony, stand at attention. The judge, a female arctic fox in an all-business blue pantsuit, meets my eyes and gives me a subtle nod of acknowledgement.

I stand self-consciously in front of Bacchus as the judge runs through the pleasantries. Bacchus has an uncanny ability to remain statuesque, his chest rising and falling almost imperceptibly. "Just relax and hold tight. Your turn will come soon enough."

The pony starts doing some tricks on the other side of the room. I don't pay much attention, instead sitting down and licking myself. Running my tongue through the denser tufts of fur around my wrists and ankles calms my mind and prevents me from feeling too self-conscious. As the clopping rings louder in my ears, I stretch myself out to my full length, concentrating on smoothing the fur on the back of my paws down. There's a sudden jolt on my hind leg, followed by an aggrieved whinny.

Oops.

After I'm satisfied that my coat is in tip-top condition, I roll onto my back. An obstacle course now fills the middle of the room. I mischievously smile at the pony as her trainer pulls her to her feet. The pup excitedly barks before shooting into the obstacle course like he's been whipped from a slingshot. I roll my eyes and then go back to my business. Just before my tongue makes contact with my fur, I spot a bright blue handkerchief in front of the judge's patent-leather Mary Janes. I shall claim it as my own.

Taking advantage of the slack in the leash, I pounce. The handkerchief shoots backwards just before my paws close around it. The judge peers down at me, and I can catch the glint of a thin length of fishing line twirled around her index finger. "Does kitten want it?"

I rapidly nod, enthusiastically bouncing on my haunches. The judge dangles my prize just beyond my grasp. I go for it again, using my powerful legs to send myself skyward, but she's too fast. I roll, coming to rest on my feet.

Determined to seize it, I pivot on my heels, taking a few bounds and then snatching it from just in front of the judge's waist. I land on my back, running the smooth fabric over my nails. The judge winks at me before turning her attention back towards the obstacle course.

There's a loud crash of metal, like a set of cymbals falling down a staircase. I follow the judge's gaze to where the pup is sprawled out on the floor. Pity. Master bends down and gently strokes my muzzle, popping a treat on my tongue. It's different this time, a peanut butter pretzel. I chuff contently.

"That was good practice. Now the real challenge." The judge leans down, dangling a tin toy in front of me. It takes a moment for my eyes to focus, but when they do, I'm confronted with my prey, a little mouse brightly painted with reds and yellows reminiscent of the circus. With a sly smile, she inserts a polished nickel key into the back and gives it a few twists. The ticking of the internal clockwork fills my ears. Once it touches the floor, it races off with surprising speed.

Not fast enough to evade a kitten, though. I move after it on all fours, laser-focusing my eyes on my target. It moves quickly on the polished hardwood floor, and I find myself relying on my front paws to keep adequate traction, my hooves threatening to slip out from under me. Despite the impediment to my acceleration, I manage to steadily gain ground on it, the thrill of the chase keeping my heart pumping fast. But as soon as I think I've gotten my paws around it, the toy blasts to the right with a *whoosh* of compressed air. My paws wrap around nothingness and I land with my butt pointed towards the ceiling, flustered.

The toy mouse scurries back towards the judge, seemingly taunting me. I snarl, breathing hard as I keep up the pursuit. I almost manage to snatch it by the pup, but he casually nudges it slightly off course while I pounce. I miss it by inches. I take a second to hiss at him before I spot it again, circling the judge's feet. I bound towards her, and this time no fancy tricks stop me. I adjust my angle as soon as I see the mouse shoot to the left. My pounce lands true. I wrap my muzzle around its metal body as the gears grind to a halt.

I turn and drop in front of my Master's feet to show off my conquest, beaming with pride. Bacchus rewards me with another sweet treat. I savor it as he wipes it off and hands it back to the judge. "Now, for the pleasure round. Are you prepared to try something a little more erotic?"

I nod, holding my head high. "I'm ready." The vixen slowly undoes the polished tortoiseshell buttons of her jacket as she looks seductively at me.

She places a soft paw on my muzzle, gently caressing my lips with her pawpads. "This is the pleasure round. You earn full points if we both walk away satisfied." Her button-down and pants slide off her body like snowmelt, revealing the pure white fur underneath. A winter coat in full bloom accentuates the curves of her body. She's a little chubby, as I'd expect for her species. Her breasts are plump, and I rise up off my haunches to teasingly paw at her areolas.

"Her name is Venus. Have fun, kitten." Bacchus hands my leash to her and then steps away. Venus leans down and coos at me as I fondle her breasts. Her eyes are clear and bright, and her scent is dominant but far less pungent, like an arctic breeze blowing over a taiga forest.

"You're Princess, hmm? Bacchus has told me all about you." Her paws move slowly down my chest until she reaches my navel. Her lipstick tastes like blackberries. She presses another treat into my muzzle, leaving her finger pressed against my lips. "If you're a good kitten for me, I'll keep the treats coming."

She gently tugs the leash upward, snapping her fingers. A plush leather chaise appears behind her, carried by two pups in rubber bodysuits. The vixen slides her panties down and spreads herself on the couch, resting her head on a plush tartan pillow. "Come on, Princess! Come here, kitten. Master has need of you."

She dangles a treat in front of her pussy, gesturing for me to come hither. I can't resist a treat. Focused on her, I calmly climb on top, resting the seat of my panties against her muzzle. Her paws slide them down to give her tongue the access it needs. For a moment I feel the cool air of the room against my slit before the hot wetness of her tongue replaces it. My thighs quiver as the vixen goes to work, her vulpine tongue pitter-pattering on my clit.

I moan and reciprocate, carefully parting the thick, fluffy fur around her slit and burying my muzzle in it. I treat it like the saucer of milk, using quick, rapid laps to make her squirm. She tastes rich and milky with a hint of salt. Up close her scent is more pungent, thick with musky arousal that tickles my nostrils.

She doesn't say anything, but I can tell when I hit the sweet spot. As her scent becomes more complex, with hints of my favorite perfume, I modify my technique, taking deep, long licks like I'm grooming my own fur. This isn't the quick and dirty process I catch out of the corner of my eye, the pup going to town on the pony doggy style. As a civilized kitten, I keep my dignity as I feel my core tremble, her experienced tongue filling my mind with lurid ecstasy.

Just before I explode onto her tongue, she pauses. Her index claw traces the contours of my clit. The arousal in my core has me taut as piano wire. "Does my kitten like being groomed?" Her voice is husky and dominant, making me eager to please her. I purr in assent before going back to my work.

"Time for your treat." Taking advantage of the natural juices built up from my arousal, she slides her fingers into me. I feel like a kitten who's gotten into the catnip. I quiver and whine as the pressure in my core increases, her tender touch causing my hips to buck as my eyes roll skyward. I'm licking almost on instinct now, my conscious mind subsumed beneath the waves of animalistic pleasure. "There we go. Feels good, doesn't it?"

I moan and feel myself tighten around her. I'm close. She leans forward until her chin rests on the nape of my neck. "Come on, kitten…cum for Master."

I whine and lick faster as orgasm washes over me like a tidal wave. As my body quivers, I shove my muzzle as deep into her as I can manage. Venus lets out a high-pitched vulpine whine and then holds my head in place, clamping her thighs together. Her juice is sweet and rich, like fresh cream. Venus stabilizes me until I've panted my last, sliding out from under me and leaving me sprawled out under the couch. She tosses me another treat as a pup starts cleaning me up with a hot towel.

I could get used to the life of a pampered kitten.

Lucky

I kick back on the patio and sip on my Killer Bee as a cool tropical breeze sways the palms clustered around the swimming pool below. Clad in bikinis and speedos, the crowd lounges on brightly-colored inflatables in a variety of shapes. A staff member bangs away on a steel drum, filling the air with Caribbean music. I have to say, when my boyfriend proposed a weekend getaway at a kink resort on a private island in the Bahamas, I expected something a lot seedier. This place is the lap of luxury.

"Another cocktail, sir?" A mouse in a French maid outfit winks at me as he slides the patio door open. His dress is hemmed short, showcasing the large bulge in his lace-trimmed panties.

"I'll take a cappuccino, and don't forget the extra foam, or there will be…consequences," I reply playfully. I catch the barest hint of a blush through his cream-colored fur as he turns and retreats the way he came. Who knew so many people had a thing for being dolled up like a French maid and ordered around?

I barely have time to return to people watching before my boyfriend, Dallas, taps on the glass. I wave for him to join me. I notice there's a patch of fur under his shark-tooth necklace that's slightly singed, and then recall he went off to the fire play seminar about two hours ago. I'm glad he had fun.

"You realize the competition is at five, right?"

My smartwatch dings. Oh yeah, I'd forgotten I'd signed up for it when we'd checked in. The otter at the main desk told me I could win a comped stay if I came out on top in the pet play competition. I leave my drink half-finished on the patio and use my watch to delay the delivery of my coffee until six. I still want to play with that mouse afterwards.

"Yeah, I haven't forgotten. Just thought I'd have a little tonic, for the nerves." I unzip my suitcase and stare for a moment at my mask. It's modeled after a German Shepherd, mostly tan leather with a single strip of black on the muzzle. The sleek leather bodysuit is neatly folded underneath it, ready to complete my transformation from Josh Barnes, C.P.A., to Lucky, pup extraordinaire.

"You ready?" My otter's sea-green eyes look me over as I unbutton my kitschy Hawaiian print shirt and cargo shorts and replace them with tight, form-fitting leather. My bodysuit feels a little more constricting around the midriff than the last time I'd donned it. I make a note to avoid the dessert bar at the buffet for the rest of my vacation. One too many crème brûlées seem to have caught up with me.

"Yeah. Are you?" Dallas rummages around in the top dresser drawer until he comes up with a chunky leather collar. The circular tag is titanium, laser engraved with "LUCKY" in Romanesque block capitals. I let him fasten it around my neck as he shoves me onto the bed.

"Of course, pup. Master is always ready to play." He shoots me a grin before lowering the mask onto my head. A moment later, after fastening the snaps and buckles, he steps back to admire his work. The black mirror in the entertainment center confirms that I am no longer a fluffy Maine Coon. "Does puppy need anything before we go for a walk?"

I whine a little, looking out at the perspiring glass left abandoned just outside. Dallas's eyes track mine. "Puppy's still thirsty?"

I nod, and Dallas snaps his fingers. The floor-to-ceiling bookcase across from the kitchenette silently swings open. It's another maid, a lynx this time. He kneels down, placing a stainless-steel doggy dish filled with a pale green liquid in front of me. As he turns away, my boyfriend flips up his skirt. I look down, sticking my muzzle into the dish and eagerly lapping the liquid up. To my delight, it's lemon-lime Gatorade. I can hear embarrassed moans of pleasure from above, but that's not my concern. I'm just a pup, and Master has the right to pleasure himself as he wishes.

Master's paws work at my crotch as I lap up the last few dregs. Something cold slides over my barbs, sending a pleasant jolt running up my cock. It envelops my entire shaft. Judging by the pressure the knot places on my pubic mound, I assume that's the canine sleeve. I shake my shoulders a little to release the nervous arousal as Master fastens it into place. "Can't have my pup going out with a cock looking like that, now can we?" He winks as he shoos the maid away.

I roll over, and he lightly strokes my belly before taking control of the leash. "Come on, pup. It's your time to shine." Crawling on my paws and knees is made slightly less awkward by the thick padding integrated into my bodysuit. I wouldn't describe is as comfortable, but it's certainly tolerable for the short distance from our room to the elevator.

"What floor?" A fennec in a brilliant red dress looks at Master and then down at me. "You heading to the competition, too?"

"Yeah! Ballroom, please," Master replies. I see the B button is already lit. "Are you one of the pets?"

The fennec shakes her head, wrapping an arm around the German Shepherd standing meekly next to her, a duffel bag tucked under her arm. "No, I'm a trainer. This little girl here is my pony, and while she may look unassuming now, she'll be a star once we get her bridled and saddled up."

I cautiously sniff at her leg. She reeks of canine. Some players go further than I do and even douse themselves in the pheromones of their species, but I've always found the smell a little difficult to handle. The German Shepherd leans over and scritches behind my ears. "He's a sweet boy. What's his name?"

"Lucky," Master replies, patting my head. I thump my leg in pleasure. The elevator doors ding open, and they head the other way down the hall towards the dressing rooms. After a short walk, Master checks his watch and brings me to heel just before the entrance to the ballroom. "Hang in there, bud. We're a little early. I don't wanna be the first ones out."

I obediently lean back on my haunches, my tail slowly sweeping back and forth. Dallas exudes dominant energy. As I sniff at the scent glands in his free paw, the pheromones put me at ease, wiping my mind free of any anxiety. He is firmly in control, and my place is to follow his lead. After a few particularly exuberant sniffs, Dallas takes notice and slowly massages the crown of my head. I start to purr before his paw stops and I realize my feline nature has slipped through. I quickly change back to a low whine and the stroking resumes.

Clip Clop. Clip Clop. I turn, and the fennec from the elevator strides past us with her pony. Master confidently grips the leash and we turn to follow her. The lights are dazzlingly bright, but I can still make out the silhouettes of a large crowd gathered to enjoy the festivities. I suppose we're tonight's entertainment.

We take our place between the other two competitors. The kitten, some breed of horse, sneers at me and goes back to grooming herself, running her tongue up and down the fur around her wrist. I start to growl, but Master taps me firmly on the head while clicking his tongue. "Lucky. Stay."

I whine a little, but keep my focus straight ahead. Fortunately, my mask blocks out my peripheral vision so I don't have to see my feline rival flaunting. The judge barks instructions I don't pay attention to, and then the horse suddenly veers off and starts trotting across the ballroom with the cacophony of a renaissance fair.

The judge seems more interested in her clipboard than the pony, although she does briefly look up when she breaks into a full gallop. I'd probably break one of my legs attempting that. I close my eyes for a moment, and when I open them the horse is on the floor and the cat is staring at her with a devious smirk.

"Lucky!" Master barks. I snap to attention. "Follow!" He leans down and unbuckles my leash before pivoting around. Behind us, an agility course has been assembled, a variety of brightly colored obstacles laid out across the center of the ballroom. I bounce up and down eagerly, barking with excitement. Master claps his paws as the judge drops a handkerchief from her outstretched paw. Now this is a challenge.

I move quickly to close the distance between me and the hurdles. Once I get close, I switch to a duck walk. It's a little awkward, but by using the powerful hind muscles built for pouncing prey, I'm able to launch myself over them before pivoting to land on my feet. Felines do have a distinct advantage in that department. I drop back down to my paws and knees as I ascend a steep ramp, which is fortunately covered with enough abrasive tape that I don't need to extend my claws to climb it. I reach nearly fifteen feet in the air before I start back down. There's no time to savor the experience.

Master claps his paws with excitement as he jogs with me. I jump another set of hurdles before I reach the weave poles. It's a little disorienting to cut back and forth through them at high speed, and by the end I have to pause for moment to prevent the room from spinning too quickly.

"Lucky! Lucky! Come on, pup!" Master's call immediately catches my attention. He motions me towards a bright purple accordion tunnel. I shake my head to clear my vision and then bound towards it. The tunnel is too short for me to crawl, so I drop to prone and wiggle along through it like a caterpillar. I'm through in thirty seconds or so.

The final obstacle confronts me like the Eye of Sauron. A giant flaming circus hoop glows a few feet above the floor, a little taller than the hurdles. All eyes are on me.

"Come on, pup! You can do it!" Master belts out a high-pitched whistle and I release, sending myself four feet high through the hoop. I quickly roll and recover, although the scent of singed headfur tells me I might have slightly overshot the jump.

One last hurdle. Simple. I charge my legs again and leap, but the pony casually kicks the bar upward as I launch. Fuck. It's too late to adjust course as I collide with the bar. It clatters on wood while I go down hard on the gymnastic mat.

Master quickly runs over and squats down next to me, his brow furrowed with concern. "Lucky. Are you okay, bud?"

I let out an indignant bark and then get back on my knees, a little bruised but no worse for wear. I glare at the pony, who's back to being groomed by her trainer with a soft terry towel. Master leans over and rubs noses with me, firmly grasping my cheeks. Everything is right with the world again. "You did such a good job for Master!"

I wag and zone out as the otter gives me affection. I tune my surroundings out until I hear the word "pleasure" from the judge. I suddenly snap back to attention.

Master reattaches my leash and points towards the pony. Her trainer is freeing her from her saddle. "Alright boy. Time to mount the pony like a good stable pup. I'll give you a little help to get you ready, okay?"

I whine as Master leads me over to her. She's on all-fours on top of a little pile of blankets and pillows, waving her rear like a tantalizing treat. I sniff at her slit, enjoying the earthy and slightly floral scent of her arousal. I move to mount her, but her trainer holds up a paw and gestures for me to retreat for a moment. I back off, letting the fennec take care of the foreplay.

Master's deft paw unzips my fly, revealing my sheathed cock. It's already half erect from the display in front of me, though the sleeve adds substantially to my size. He nods approvingly at it as he runs his paw up and down the shaft, teasing the delicate cock inside. I whine as his other paw holds tight to the leash. Master works with a mustelid slyness, his exertions causing the arousal churning in the pit of my stomach to shoot up my spine. Once he deems me ready, he cracks open a tube of lubricant and applies a generous dollop to my cock, spreading it all over to ensure I'm slicked up for the mare's pleasure, not that she needs it with the way she's dripping.

The pony's trainer climbs off her and gives me a finger wag. I bark and close the distance between us in a few bounds, pausing to position myself properly once I'm right behind her. I place my paws on her shoulders, brushing her tail to the side. She raises her rear a little to give me better access to her pussy. It's been a while since I've been with a female pony, but I think I've still got the hang of the process.

I nuzzle at her neck as I start pushing inside her, feeling her body tense and then relax. The lubricant is chilly enough to feel through the thermoplastic, and it intensifies my arousal as I push into her up to the hilt of my knot. She moans and clenches around my cock. I start sliding out, the sensation on my sheath sending lightning up my spine.

Something primal in me activates, and I transition to shorter, quicker thrusts, angling myself so the knot of my cock grinds against her clit. She moans and whines as I feel a sudden pressure under my tail. *Zip*. I feel Master's index finger, freezing with lubricant, gently circling my asshole. As I do my duty as a stable pup, Master offers his reward. His fingers stimulate me from behind in tandem with my thrusts into her.

It's almost too much, but I restrain myself until I feel the mare buckle beneath me, overwhelmed with orgasmic bliss. I give one more thrust and then jam myself all the way inside her as my cock explodes. My load, built up from a day of teasing and foreplay, fills her up totally, rebounding and coating my shaft in warm, sticky release.

All in a day's work for a stable pup.

Phoenix

The bit is ice cold as Nila slides it into my muzzle. Clad in a sparkling dress the color of wildfire, the lithe fennec deftly fastens the bridle, pulling the straps tight across my cheeks and forehead. The long mirror on the dressing room vanity reveals my transformation from humble German Shepherd to elegant equestrian champion. This isn't my first rodeo. I flex my cheeks, adjusting the bridle until it rests comfortably on the silicone caps fitted over my back teeth.

The riding outfit leaves my breasts bare, supple black leather running in thick strips down the middle of my tan coat to provide support for the elaborate saddle fastened around my midriff. It's thick and substantial, decorated with turquoise and freshly polished silver. It glints in the incandescent light as I twirl around. It was a hell of a challenge convincing the flight attendant it was my carry-on.

"Down." Nila taps my ass with the end of her leather riding crop. I take a knee to make it easier for her to make adjustments. The dressing room smells faintly of roses, and my stomach growls for a morsel of Turkish delight.

"Good girl!" Something sweet is pressed into my muzzle. It doesn't quite edge out the vaguely metallic flavor of the bit, but the sugar cube is welcome nonetheless. There's a firm pressure on my forehead, and then a loud click as she fastens the crownpiece. Nila steps back to admire her work. I rise, my transformation complete. The hoof boots give me enough of a boost in height I could just about rest my chin on the tips of her ears. Her ruby earrings look like morsels of tangerine. I lean forward and playfully bite at one.

"No!" She shakes her head, slapping my ass with the crop. "Phoenix, walk," she says with authority. Grasping my reigns tightly, she guides me towards the door. I immediately sense the shift in power as Nila assumes her position as my trainer. Her tennis shoes squeak softly with each step.

Nila stays close behind me, paw darting out to push the door aside just before my muzzle touches it. It's a short journey down a service hallway to the grand ballroom. Dozens of kinksters line the multi-tiered seating around the central floor, lounged on tasteful earth-toned furniture. They're busy engaging in bouts of foreplay before the show begins. My heart starts pounding in my chest as I see lazy eyes turn to me, drawn by my plume glimmering like a disco ball. Once more unto the breach.

We're the first to present ourselves, and Nila halts me in the center with a gentle tug of the reins. The judge sits just a few feet in front of us, an elegant arctic fox vixen in a form-fitting blue pantsuit and vintage horn-rimmed eyeglasses. She's sprawled on a black leather couch, chewing on the cap of her pen as she scribbles something on a clipboard.

"Lucky, heel!" An otter with a chic shark-tooth necklace stops to our left. His pup looks curiously at me, some sort of feline hidden under a leather hood. I get a little chill when I realize he's imitating my own species. He drops onto all fours, tail wagging excitedly. He's not quite perfect, but his body language is a reasonably good imitation of the real thing.

A delicate mewl from further to port grabs my attention. The kitten is a strapping Arabian mare, her muscular body covered only by a sports bra and bright pink panties. Her ears have been covered over with fuzzy prosthetics, calico faux fur standing out against her gray coat. A shiny silver bell dangles from her rhinestone-studded collar.

The judge rises from the sofa and tweaks her glasses. Her lipstick is electric purple, making the tip of her muzzle look like a tiny plum as she purses her lips. "Welcome, competitors. My name is Venus, and I'll be performing evaluations this evening." She takes a few steps forward, her tall high heels clacking on the heavily-lacquered mahogany floor. "First, the species-specific evaluation."

She pauses in front of me, eyes locked on my trainer. "She is a show pony, yes?"

"And a pleasure pony as well," Nila replies. My cheeks flush, though I'm sure my dark ruffs disguise any visible blush.

"Good. First, the visual inspection." The vixen's paw snaps to attention, stopping just above my right breast. I give her a little nod to proceed. Her fingers gently circle my areola before cupping my breast. I try not to fidget, although the sensation awakens the low heat of arousal pulsing in my core. She slyly grins at me before turning to Nila. "Her coat is excellent. Breasts are firm and well-proportioned." She squats down, a measuring tape springing from her sleeve. She tugs on my tail prosthesis, and I clench a little to hold it in place. "Tail four inches from the bottom of the hock."

Venus steps back, satisfied, before scribbling on her clipboard. "Excellent. Trainer, will you please have her demonstrate the proper gaits?"

Nila pulls on the reins, the pressure on the bit turning me to the right. "Walk! Yah!" She lightly slaps my ass with the riding crop. I move forward at a moderate pace, my feet clip-clopping on the hardwood. I hold my head high, squinting a little to keep the bright stage lights from searing my corneas.

"Canter!" Another slap. I take a deep breath. Canter is awkward on two legs. I quicken my pace and modify my gait so there's a brief moment where both my legs are suspended in empty air. I recall falling flat on my face on my first few attempts. I focus on keeping my balance, the gel padding of the boots squishing with each step. The crowd is silhouetted, my mental energy focused on maintaining the perfect regulation pace. Just before I reach the first row of spectators, Nila tugs hard on the reins. "Whoa, girl!"

I take a few more steps to catch my balance and then halt, my heart pounding in my ears. The musk of the crowd is strong here, forcing me to grit my teeth to avoid a burst of arousal disrupting my concentration. Nila steers me around until I'm pointed back at the other competitors. "Gallop! Yah!" She slaps me hard, and I whinny in surprise before moving at full steam. The air rushes through my mane as it trails behind me. I gallop like a wild Mustang, moving with such abandon that Nila starts tugging on the reins to slow my pace.

My vision tunnels to just the judge ahead of me. The air is pleasantly cool, dispersing the heat radiating from my fur. I could do this all day.

Without warning, a hard tug jolts me back to reality. I try and slow myself down as I notice the kitten directly in my path. Like a fully loaded locomotive, I can't stop in time. The kitten takes my legs out from under me. I go flying to the ground, plume breaking off my bridle and soaring somewhere into the crowd. A moment later, I hear an indignant shout.

"Tsk, so close to a perfect score." The vixen flashes pearly white teeth. Nila helps me to my feet, dusting me off with a damp towel. I stand at attention, trying not to display my shame as the judge takes the other two pets through their paces. I envy the kitten. Her task looks far less demanding than maintaining a trot in unnatural hoof boots. Having to catch a toy mouse; come on. At least it passes quickly.

Clap. Clap. Clap. "Well done, competitors! This concludes the individual evaluations. Now, for the pleasure round."

The judge walks over to the kitten as Nila hugs me close for a moment. She's a little muskier now from exertion. Something sweet pops into my mouth. It's rich and creamy once I bite through the hard outer layer. Belgian seashells; my one weakness. The chocolate quickly drowns out the metallic bite of the bit, slowing my heartbeat back to something approaching normal.

The pup's trainer leads him over to me. He's a Maine Coon from the looks of the long, tufted fur jutting through the collar between his mask and sleek leather bodysuit. I recognize him from the elevator. His name is Lucky. The otter keeps him close as Nila's slender fingers work at the buckles around my mons pubis. A weight drops off my lower back. Nila catches the saddle before it touches the floor, stepping back and handing it off to an oryx in black tie.

I'm bare underneath the saddle. A delicate breeze flows across my pussy, sending a shiver through my core. The crowd looks intently toward us as the pup's trainer unzips the front of his bodysuit. A bright red sheath with a hefty knot at the base lolls out. I suppose the pup play outfit isn't complete without anatomically correct equipment.

"And now, a demonstration of a service pup breeding the mare. Full points are awarded only if they both achieve orgasm!"

Like a veteran ringmaster, the judge draws the crowd's attention before turning her focus back to the kitten.

Two more service pups appear from a secondary entrance, carrying foam pads, pillows, and blankets. They're tossed haphazardly on the floor, spread out like a stable in winter. The pup crawls over to me on paws and knees, pausing to nose at my pussy. The sensation of leather on my clit makes me thighs jitter with tension. I take a deep breath and bend down, adjusting my position until I feel sufficient cushioning underneath me. I don't have the benefit of built in padding like he does.

"Shh...shh..." I feel Nila's warm paw rest on my ass as her muzzle makes contact with mine. Her breath smells like cinnamon chewing gum and I'm sure her bright red lipstick leaves a stain on my fur. She retakes possession of my reins and holds me in position, her tongue running across my top teeth. I moan softly as one of her fingers pushes into me. "Be a good pony for your trainer."

She pulls away and flips her leg over my back, positioned so she's straddling me bareback as her fingers dance around inside of me, slick with my natural juices. Her weight is comforting, her dominant energy allowing me to relax out as my paws curl around a spotted comforter. She keeps stimulating me until I imagine I'm practically dripping onto the blankets below. Behind me, I hear the click of a plastic container opening, and then a wet spurt. Nila gets off of me, softly brushing my forehead with her soft lips. "Trainer wants you to be good for the service pup. Make sure he has fun."

I whinny softly in response as something cold presses against my clit. That must be the sheath. The pup places his paws on my shoulders, nuzzling the nape of my neck with his leather nose. I grunt a little as he pushes into me. The sheath looked smaller than it feels, though it warms up as he works his way inside. As soon as it feels like he's in me as far as the bulb of the knot, he quickly eases out and then pushes back in. I bite my lip and neigh in pleasure.

For a cat, he's surprisingly adept at doggy style. His motions are primal, and I clench my pelvic muscles around the shaft to feel the full girth of the canine sleeve. Like a mare in estrus I whine with need, looking ahead as Nila gradually strips for me, revealing the taut curves of her body. An employee appears behind her to place a large velvet armchair down. She plops down in just her bra and red silk panties.

The pup playfully bites at my mane while I watch Nila's delicately manicured nails slide down the front of her underwear. She stares teasingly at me, and out of the corner of my eye I notice the judge has shed her suit in order to play with the kitten.

The pressure in my core slowly builds, an electric tingle that runs up my spine and forces me to buck my hips in tandem with his thrusts. I'm a feral mare now, the pup aggressively slamming into me with each thrust. Nila has shut her eyes, the front of her panties damp with arousal as she pleasures herself.

The pup barks, nuzzling my neck, panting with exertion. I can sense he's close. I am, too. I whinny as the sheath grinds against my clit. Like the snapping of a bowstring, the release comes without warning. It overwhelms me like a tsunami, turning my arms to gelatin. As I collapse to the ground, I feel Nila's strong arm rest in between my breasts. Her other paw works at her pussy as the pup gives a final push to force his knot into me.

The warmth quickly fills me up as I drop onto the nest of blankets, panting loudly as the pup collapses on top of me. I feel the pup instinctively tug to withdraw, but a bioreactive in the knot has inflated it fully in response to his orgasm. He's trapped in me for a moment until it deflates. Nila leans over and gently scratches behind my ears. "You've been a very good pleasure pony, Phoenix. You did so well for your trainer."

The judge buttons up her jacket as Nila plops another chocolate onto my tongue. Polishing her lenses of her classes with a microfiber cloth, she appears bemused at the sight of the pup flopped on the blanket pile. She grabs her clipboard from where she'd left it on the sofa and makes a few quick checkmarks with her pen. Nila grasps the reins as the judge clears her throat.

"*Hem-hem.*" Nila's eyes flick upward. "I am pleased to announce that after tallying the results, all three competitors have a score of ninety-eight points. We have a three-way tie." She taps the pen against the clipboard. "Each of you were so close to perfect. Just one little mistake."

Nila cocks an eyebrow. "So, what does that mean?"

The judge chuckles. "I think you've all given us enough of a show to earn a free stay. Go and enjoy the festivities."

The crowd gives us a round of applause. I notice staff passing out towels and wet wipes. Seems like we weren't the only ones who enjoyed ourselves.

I grasp Nila's paw and let her lift me to my feet as I bathe in orgasmic afterglow. "Let's get you cleaned up and brushed. The other trainers want to do a little get together on the beach, if you're interested."

"As long as I get a bubble bath first, I'm down for anything." I blush as cum drips down my inner thigh, my fur reeking of musk.

Nila chuckles and leads me towards the exit. "You can have anything your heart desires, sweetheart. You've earned it, my little prize-winning pony."

"I have to say, I didn't expect this vacation to be free." Bella leans back, kicking her feet up on the padded blue and white striped footstool. She snaps her fingers, and a wolf arrives with her hot sake on a silver platter. "Are you all enjoying the resort as much as I am?"

"I fear I'm turning into a lotus-eater." Nila takes a piece of sushi off the nude fennec in the middle and pops it into her mouth. "They really do indulge your every desire here. I'm not the only one that's done some really kinky shit, right?"

"Of course not; isn't that the point of coming here?" Dallas swirls his Jack Daniels and slams it down in one gulp. "Having a submissive pup to enjoy it with isn't too bad either."

In the cool evening air, the pets play on the white sand beach while their Masters enjoy dinner, the palms gently swaying in the sea breeze.

Another successful evening at the Isla del Placer.

Bïos

LINNEA "LITERALGRILL" CAPPS is a three-time August Derleth award winning poet and Leo Literary Award winning author. She's also a smoking hot grill on the internet and would absolutely give any good pup the BEST belly rubs, just ask~ When not dangling strings in front of cute kittens, she plays songs on her ukulele and writes the stories she dreams up before bed every night. You can find her on Twitter @LiteralGrill and on her website www.linneacapps.com.

JADEN DRACKUS, or Jay Dee is a dragnox from Maryland. He has been a good pupper and writing furry stories since 2010 and writing for publication since 2016. A historian by training, he was inspired in his youth by science fiction and fantasy, he tends to work in those genres as well as historical fiction when he writes.

He lives with 4 cats. Playing video and card games, building plastic models, and reading make Jay Dee waggy. Recently, he has begun experimenting with being a hyno fox (his take on pup play). He is an alumnus of the Regional Anthropomorphic Writers Retreat. In 2019, he was a very good boy and earned a Leo Literary Award for Best Short Story.

His stories can be seen in *Breeds: Wolves* from THP Bound Tales and *Fang 8,9,* and *10* from FurPlanet. He can be found on FurAffinity as JadenDrackus. His silly observations on life can be seen on Twitter: @JadenDrakus.

Hmm? Oh, no, I'm not a puppy. I prefer to watch them play and have fun from a distance. I can't resist petting the occasional boy or girl when they come for me for attention though. Perhaps I'll even take one home with me tonight. Who knows?

FAOLAN is an otter residing in the Netherlands, where he spends his daytime being an English teacher, and his night-time working on his hobbies, consisting of dancing, writing, gaming, watching various series, browsing the internet for things he doesn't need, taking care of his fish, and taking care of his pet snake. His stories are featured in other THP books, such as *Seven Deadly Sins, Infurno, Purrgatorio, Species/Breeds: Wolves,* and *Slashers.*
https://twitter.com/FaolanPanriel

After moving to Ohio, **TJ** found the furry fandom. It's there that, after a few motivators, the rat had the urge to pick up a pen – or grab a keyboard, as it more often is these days. Since then, he's been creating characters, writing stories, and started a novel. The more he's written, the more friends he's made though different writing circles. When not focusing on words, TJ enjoys other nerdy activities, like Magic: the Gathering, tabletop RPGs, and video games. More recently, he's found a new way to relax as a hypno-pup.

TJ's other stories may be found in issues of *FANG, Heat* and other anthologies both in and out of the fandom. For thoughts, comments and replies in bite-sized chunks, he can be found on Twitter @TJMinde.

AL SONG is a red kangaroo living near the caffeine-fueled city of Seattle, which houses the wondrous, gay, erotic goods retailer, Dog House Leathers. This incredible store, along with the internet introduced and informed the roo about the world of pup play.

When the roo isn't writing he enjoys playing his viola, flute, and guitar. He also loves escape rooms and learning different languages. He studied German and comparative literature in college and hopes to get a novel published one day.

If you want to read more of his stories he's in the

anthologies: *Fang 8, Roar 9, Tales from the Guild: World Tour, The Furry Cookbook, Foxers or Beariefs, Sensory De-Tails, Difursity: Stories by Furries of Color,* along with the upcoming *Howloween.*

You can also find him at:

-FurAffinity: **www.furaffinity.net/user/alsong/**
-SoFurry: **https://alsong.sofurry.com/**
-Twitter: @song_roo

THOMAS "FAUX" STEELE is a native Virginian well-versed in kink fiction. While "The Competition" is his first published story to feature pet play, he has had plenty of practice being a master for his corgi, Auggie, to whom this story is dedicated. He's an arctic fox whose stories have been published in numerous anthologies and conbooks including Fang 7, Dogs of War Volume II, and Boldly Going Forward. When not hunkered down in the law library, he enjoys driving German cars, exploring exotic locales, and bribing his puppy to do tricks with gummy bears. You can find more of his work at **furaffinity.net/user/fauxhammer**.

For THIGER, what came first between furry and puplay is a bit like the chicken or the egg question; they were always there. Whatever the case, he's been enjoying making pups enjoy themselves for years, and currently owns a very nice cat. You can find more like this in Electric Sewer, Vol 1, or see his art over at @Thiger_art.

www.ingramcontent.com/pod-product-compliance
Lightning Source LLC
Chambersburg PA
CBHW071438260626
47170CB00008B/2762